RANGER FAITH

TEXAS RANGER HEROES

LYNN SHANNON

CT
Creative Thoughts

This novel is dedicated to anyone who has struggled after a traumatic incident. May you find peace, love, and strength.

He heals the brokenhearted and binds up their wounds.

ONE

He was going to kill her.

Emilia Sanchez ran through the woods, her bare feet slipping over the pine needles and leaves. Her calf burned from a stab wound. Rope dangled from one wrist and the cuts on her forearm were bleeding. Frigid air sank into her skin. Her blouse and skirt were little protection from the December night, but there hadn't been time to grab anything heavier before escaping from the hunting cabin.

She was lucky to have the cell phone. And her life.

Emilia stumbled. Her knees hit the hard earth with a jolt. The world swam before her eyes. She'd been drugged during the initial kidnapping, and the medications were wreaking havoc with her coordination. She sucked in a desperate breath and blinked to clear her vision.

"Emilia, my pet." The singsong voice came from some place behind her. "You've been a baaaaad girl."

She glanced over her shoulder, a scream rising in her throat. A shadow shifted. Man-sized. Big enough to be the serial killer who'd captured her. Emilia was intimately familiar with his crimes. As a trained behavioral analyst, she'd been requested by the task force to create a profile of the killer. She'd seen the crime scene photos of the previous victims, studied the cases.

Three women. Dark-haired. Pretty. Unmarried. All had been sliced with a knife in an intricate pattern before being stabbed through the heart. Emilia hadn't known she would become the killer's next target.

Victim number four.

"Oh, Emilia....don't run, my pet."

His laughter surrounded her. He was close. Too close. Panic rose, threatening to crush her, but she battled it back. Her hand tightened around the cell phone. Help was a call away. She just needed to get to a place with cell service. *Please, God, give me strength.*

Emilia struggled to her feet. Blood ran down her leg from the wound in her calf and a sharp pain accompanied every step. She ignored it, weaving and dodging deeper into the woods. An owl hooted above her. In the distance, a lake shimmered in the moonlight.

Where was she? Emilia had no idea. Someplace remote.

She paused, leaning against a tree. Her breath came in gasps. She tried to listen for the killer, but it was too hard to hear anything over the pounding of her heart. Should she check for cell service? It was risky. The light could give her position away, but without help, she wouldn't survive.

Emilia clicked the side button. The screen glowed. One bar.

Relief made her knees weak. The cell phone wasn't hers, but thankfully it didn't require a passcode to access the keypad. She could call 9-1-1 but it would take too much time to explain her circumstances to dispatch. Instead, she punched in a familiar number. Texas Ranger Bennett Knox was her colleague, and they'd formed a close friendship over the last few weeks while working the murder cases together.

Emilia's fingers shook as she hit the call button. Blood from the wounds on her arm dripped onto her hand and the phone. She glanced over her shoulder. Moonlight filtered through the trees, casting eerie shapes. There was no sign of the killer, but that didn't mean he wasn't close. The sour taste of fear filled her mouth.

"Knox."

His voice was brisk and authoritative. Inexplicable tears flooded Emilia's eyes. "B-B-Bennett. The killer—"

"I know, Emilia. Where are you?"

Concern and fear layered his tone. Bennett must've been looking for her. How long had she been missing? Emilia had lost all sense of time.

She licked her dry lips. Shudders overtook her body as an icy wind snaked around her petite form and cut through her thin clothes. "I don't know where I am. In the woods. There's a lake. Can you trace this phone number and get a GPS lock on me?"

"Already doing it."

Indistinct voices filtered over the line. It sounded like Bennett was in the Fulton County Sheriff's Department. How far away was Emilia from help? Would they be able to reach her in time?

There were things Bennett needed to know. Emilia glanced behind her again, checking for movement. "Bennett, the killer is Derrick Jackson."

The Texas Ranger inhaled sharply. Derrick had been one of their suspects, but he wasn't high on the list. Emilia scanned the surrounding area. Leaves moved in the wind. "He's hunting for me."

"Emilia, can you get to a safe place? Do you see a road? Or a house nearby?"

Pain coursed through her body. The cuts on her arm and leg were throbbing. Emilia sagged heavier against the tree. Her vision swam. Blood loss coupled with whatever drug Derrick had injected her with were taking their toll.

"I...I don't feel...I'm hurt..." She pressed a hand to her arm, but the blood rushed around her fingers. The cut was too big. Too deep. And she was so cold. Her teeth chattered.

"Hold on, Emilia. I'm coming. Just hold on."

A branch snapped. Emilia whirled as a figure slammed into her. The cell phone flew from her hand as she tumbled to the ground. The attacker landed on top of Emilia. The air whooshed from her lungs and stars danced in front of her eyes.

"There you are, my pet." A gloved hand caressed her hair. "You escaped."

Bile rose in the back of her throat. Had Derrick seen the cell phone? Did he know she'd been talking to someone? Emilia didn't think so. Otherwise, she'd be dead now. Derrick wouldn't waste time torturing her if he knew police were on the way.

"I underestimated you." Derrick leaned down and whispered in her ear. His breath was hot on her cheek. "You're better than the others."

The others. The three women he'd killed. Their faces flashed in succession before her eyes—and those were ones she knew about. There was little doubt Derrick had been killing for a long time. There were more victims.

He was a monster. And those women deserved justice.

A wave of rage mixed with the fresh course of adrenaline pumping through her veins. Emilia jabbed with her elbow, nailing her attacker in the ribs. His hold loosened. Relying on years of karate practice, she twisted away before kicking out with her good foot. The hit landed square in his gut. He fell back with a groan.

Emilia scrambled to her feet. She ran blindly as sheer survival instinct took over. Footsteps pounded behind her. It seemed the killer's breath was on her neck. Branches slapped her face and roots threatened to trip her already unsteady gait.

Suddenly the trees were gone, and the lake loomed large. She bolted, seeking cover. Somewhere. Anywhere.

The bare soles of her feet slapped against wood. Too late, Emilia realized she'd diverted onto a dock extending into the lake. The water yawned like a black hole beyond the wooden railing.

It was a dead end.

She spun. A man dressed in black stood at the end of the dock. His face was in shadows, but Emilia didn't need to see it to know he was smiling. Derrick enjoyed the fight and her fear.

He ambled closer. "We're going to have so much fun together."

Derrick lifted his hand. Moonlight bounced off the sharp blade.

Emilia's heart thundered. She glanced at the lake. The water would be icy, cold enough to cause hypothermia. That is, if she didn't drown first. A likely outcome given her weakened state.

Boots thumped against the dock as Derrick came closer.

There was no choice.

Emilia scrambled up the wooden railing. Behind her, Derrick yelled, his feet pounding harder on the dock. She felt the brush of his hand on her arm as he grabbed for her.

He missed.

She dove into the inky water.

TWO

One year later

Texas Ranger Bennett Knox hauled the Christmas tree up the porch steps. Afternoon sunshine warmed his back and the needles on the Douglas fir tickled his cheeks.

"Why do you have to be so stubborn?" Bennett's sister, Sage, marched ahead of him and opened the front door. She was dressed for the holiday season in a reindeer sweater. "It's one date."

Bennett smothered a groan of annoyance. He should've known better than to invite

Sage along to collect the Christmas tree. She'd taken the opportunity to bug him about his love life. Or rather, the lack of one. He gripped the tree trunk with his gloved hands. "For the thousandth time, I'm not interested. Stop trying to set me up with your friends."

"It's been four years since your divorce. Don't you think it's time to get back into the saddle?"

He rolled his eyes. "Dating is not the same as being thrown from a horse, Sage."

"Sure it is. You try it and get hurt. The second time is more fearful because you know

what can happen when things go wrong."

Bennett maneuvered the tree through his parents' living room before carefully placing it in the waiting stand. "In my case, horribly wrong."

His ex-wife—the woman who'd promised to love, honor, and cherish him—decided two days before their one-year anniversary that marriage wasn't for her. Bennett went to work Monday morning completely unaware of the trouble in their relationship. He came home that night to find the house devoid of furniture. All she left behind was her wedding ring and an apology letter.

"Hold the tree straight, please." Sage bent down to tighten the screws on the stand. Her slender form disappeared under the lower boughs. "I want you to be happy, Bennett. All you do is work, work, work. How are you going to meet someone if you never date?"

"I'm not interested in meeting anyone. End of story."

Sage backed out from underneath the tree and swiped at her hair. "Uh-huh. We'll see."

The back door banged open, followed by a thunderous set of footprints. Bennett braced himself as his niece raced into the living room and used the couch as a launching pad. The five-year-old slammed into his back, wrapping her slender arms around his throat. "Uncle B, Uncle B, Uncle B."

"Elizabeth Marie Hutchins!" Sage planted her hands on her hips. "Did you just jump on Nana's couch?"

"Sorry, Mama." Liz clung to Bennett. "Uncle B is too tall for me to jump on without using the couch."

Bennett smothered a laugh. Sage glared at him, but there was a twitch at the corner of her mouth as she fought to contain her own smile.

Sage cleared her throat. "I'm sure if you ask nicely next time, Uncle Bennett will bend down so you can climb on his back." She tickled her daughter's side. "You little spider monkey. Don't use Nana's couch."

"Yes, Mama." Liz leaned over so she could see Bennett's face. "Uncle B, some lady is here to see you. She's outside." Liz flashed an adorable grin. One front tooth was missing. "And she's very pretty."

Bennett rolled his eyes. "Heavens, not you too."

Sage laughed. "The apple doesn't fall far from the tree."

"Tell me about it. I'm surrounded by matchmaking females. Even Mom is getting in on the action." Bennett adjusted his hold on his niece. "Come on, Liz, let's go see who came for a visit."

He wasn't expecting anyone, but that didn't matter. People often stopped by the ranch for a chat or to discuss a problem. Liz giggled as Bennett bounced her on his back in a pony ride. His boots thumped against the front porch.

A woman was waiting on the wide driveway next to a

sedan. A silky curtain of dark hair hid her face. Duke, Bennett's German shepherd, was making himself useful as a greeting party. The dog's tail swiped across the concrete as the visitor stroked his head.

Bennett hopped down the porch stairs. "Can I help you, ma'am?"

The woman glanced up. Bennett's steps faltered. "Emilia."

They hadn't spoken in several months, hadn't seen each other in almost a year. The friendship they'd formed while working on the task force shifted after Derrick's attack on Emilia. Conversations became stiff and uneasy. Emilia never said it outright, but Bennett understood his presence triggered unwanted memories about the night she nearly died. It wasn't possible to avoid each other completely due to work, but Bennett did his best to minimize their contact to avoid causing Emilia pain.

He missed her though. Their friendship had meant something to him, and he was happy to see her now. Light makeup colored Emilia's cheeks and lips, drawing attention to her gorgeous features. Bangs flirted with chocolate-brown eyes. Her jacket was unbuttoned, and the pink sweater and slacks underneath hugged her curves.

Emilia dropped her hand from Duke's head. "Hi, Bennett. I'm sorry to drop in like this, but I need to speak to you. It's important."

"See, Uncle B." Liz announced loudly from her perch on Bennett's back. "Didn't I tell you she was pretty?"

Heat warmed the back of his neck. There was no denying Emilia was stunning, but now was not the time to discuss it. Bennett lowered his niece to the ground. "Liz, honey, go inside and help your mom find Nana's decorations."

"Okay." She waved to Emilia. "Nice to meet you again. I know you said we met before when I was four, but I don't remember."

Emilia smiled softly. "That's okay. Nice to meet you, too, Liz."

The little girl skipped inside the house. Emilia gestured after her. "Your niece is as adorable as I remember."

"She's a handful but a cute one." Bennett removed his work gloves. "And, as you can tell, as opinionated as my baby sister."

Emilia laughed. Bennett tossed the gloves in the bed of the ranch work truck. "Come on in. There's fresh coffee and my mom probably has some cookies in the jar."

"I don't want to disturb your family." Her gaze flickered to the house before settling back on him. "And what we need to discuss should be done privately."

It was becoming clear this wasn't a personal visit, but a business one. Emilia was a state police officer and behavioral analyst. She aided investigations by studying crime scenes and creating profiles of the killers. Bennett couldn't imagine what case brought her to his doorstep.

Derrick's? Couldn't be. The killer was dead.

Questions circled Bennett's mind, but he held them in. "There's no need to worry. My parents are shopping.

Sage and Liz will be busy pulling decorations down from the attic. And my brother-in-law"—he waved a hand toward the pastures—"is checking the fence line. We'll have the kitchen to ourselves."

He led her inside. The kitchen was large with an island and a plank table comfortable enough to seat twelve. Bennett removed two mugs from the rack hanging on the wall and poured coffee. "Mom doesn't have caramel creamer, but there is milk."

"Milk is fine." Emilia shrugged off her jacket and hung it on the back of a chair. She tilted her head. "You remember I like caramel creamer?"

He opened the fridge. "I'm a ranger, Emilia. It's my job to notice things."

That was a half-truth. Bennett's interest in Emilia had gone beyond his job, and there were lots of things he remembered about her. Emilia drummed her nails while thinking. She was left-handed and couldn't stand peppers on her pizza. Their friendship never shifted into romance, but Bennett had hoped it might someday. Emilia was the only woman he'd ever met that made him question his commitment to never remarry.

Bennett set the milk on the table, along with a spoon. Then he fished a few cookies out of the jar on the counter and plated them. Emilia stirred her coffee, lost in thought. Her mouth was set in a hard line and her brow crinkled.

Bennett joined her at the table. "What's going on?"

Emilia tapped her spoon against the mug. She pulled out her cell phone from the pocket of her jacket. "I was working a case near El Paso and arrived home this morning to find a flower delivery on my doorstep."

She tapped her cell phone screen and then turned it toward Bennett. His chest constricted. A poinsettia plant rested on the welcome mat. Visible above the flowers, attached to a florist stick, was a card with a typewritten message.

The murders begin again, my pet.

The significance of the threat wasn't lost on Bennett. It was a clear reference to Derrick Jackson. After killing a woman, Derrick left the body in a public park with a poinsettia bloom clutched in the victim's hands. Emilia had almost been his fourth victim. She'd escaped by diving into a lake, swimming to the other side, and crawling out. Bennett had found her near death, suffering from multiple knife wounds and hypothermia.

Anger swept through him, fast and furious. Whoever had left this on Emilia's doorstep was aiming to hurt and terrify her. Bennett tapped the cell phone screen to zoom in on the message. "Did you report this to your superiors? It's not Derrick, obviously, since he's dead. But investigators should still take it seriously. A criminal out for revenge may have researched your history and is using it to threaten you."

"I have reported it, but..." She swallowed hard. "I don't think this is from one of my other cases."

"Can you explain why?"

Emilia met his gaze and took a deep breath. "Derrick may not have been working alone."

Dread spread through Emilia like poison. Speaking her worst fears out loud made them real. She wanted to be wrong. Prayed she was. But somewhere deep in her heart, she already knew it was true. Emilia's hand trembled, and she gripped her coffee mug.

Bennett frowned. "I don't understand. You identified Derrick as your attacker."

"He kidnapped me from the parking lot. I know that for sure." Emilia licked her lips. "But later...in the cabin..."

Maybe it was her imagination, but the scar along her right arm seemed to burn. Emilia's fingers slipped inside her sleeve and she rubbed the mottled skin. "I was drugged. My memories about that night are hazy. I was certain Derrick was the one who'd cut me and chased me through the woods. After I left the hospital, I started questioning myself. The nagging feeling that I was missing something important wouldn't leave me."

Bennett sat back in his chair. His brow crinkled. "Why didn't you say something to me?"

The question had plagued her the entire drive to the ranch. Why hadn't she said anything about her suspicions? There was a laundry list of reasons, most due to her own self-doubts.

Emilia rose from the chair and crossed to the window. In the pasture, horses grazed. A white picket fence marked the property line. It was as pretty as a picture.

Peaceful. Emilia had forgotten how much she loved it here.

She hugged herself and blew out a breath. "I don't know how to explain it, Bennett. I had nightmares for months after Derrick's attack and was suffering from post-traumatic stress disorder. It was hard to separate what was real from what wasn't. Therapy helped and...I don't know. I convinced myself that a second person in the cabin was a figment of my imagination."

"Until you received this poinsettia and message on your doorstep."

She nodded. "Do you think I'm losing it?"

"No. Emilia, you have some of the best instincts of any cop I've ever worked with. And you didn't make up this message. It's clearly referencing the killings last Christmas."

She turned to face him. Bennett's auburn hair was cut short, but the look suited the sharp planes of his features. A navy jacket encased his broad shoulders. The color brought out the gold flecks in his sharp green eyes. There was no recrimination in his expression. Instead, there was sympathy and understanding.

A pang of regret pierced through the shell Emilia wrapped around her heart. She and Bennett had been close friends at one point. Family dinners on his ranch, attending church on Sunday, hours spent working the murders.

After Derrick's attack, it changed. Bennett became intrinsically linked to the case that had almost cost Emilia her life. She remembered the feel of Bennett's arms gently cradling her against his chest as he raced to the ambulance after finding her in the woods near the lake.

You're going to be okay, Em. You're a fighter. Just stay awake for me and I'll do the rest.

She'd survived many things. A no-good father, a drug-addicted mother, and more than a decade in the foster care system. Through it all, she'd persevered. But Derrick's attack damaged Emilia in a fundamental way. It nearly crippled her. All she wanted was to forget the incident and lead a normal life. Her relationship with Bennett was a causality of that decision.

Still, Emilia had regrets. There was a time she'd envisioned her friendship with Bennett would deepen into something more. A foolish school-girl dream.

"Problem is, there's no indication Derrick worked with a partner," Bennett said, jolting Emilia from her runaway thoughts. "You reviewed the case files of the first three victims and believed he was working alone."

"I did." She rubbed her forehead. "But profiling isn't an exact science, Bennett. It's helpful, but it doesn't replace hard facts. The task force was dismantled after Derrick died. How much did Sheriff King investigate after that?"

Bennett didn't answer. He didn't have to. Emilia already knew. The political pressure to solve the murders had been overwhelming. The sheriff hadn't done anything after Derrick's death except claim victory.

Emilia returned to the table and sat down. "Have there been any murders in Fulton County? Anything that might resemble the other cases?"

Bennett shook his head. "No."

The knot in Emilia's stomach loosened. Any crime like the previous murders—a woman left stabbed in a public park with a poinsettia bloom—Bennett would have knowledge of. As a Texas Ranger, he assisted with serious cases. Fulton County didn't have the resources to handle a complicated murder.

Bennett leaned back in his chair. "Let's assume you're right, Emilia. Why would the real killer wait so long before coming forward?"

She pointed to the poinsettia in the photograph. "These plants are seasonal. They only bloom from October to January. All the murders last year happened at Christmastime. Something about the holidays may trigger the killer."

The media had dubbed him the Holiday Slasher. The nickname was particularly fitting if her theory was correct.

Bennett's mouth hardened. "You're a target, Emilia. The one who got away. This message is designed to bring you back to Fulton County."

"Except if the plan was merely to kill me, he could've accomplished that already. He wants something else."

"What?"

"I don't know." She ran a hand through her hair. It was her job to create a profile of the killer, but this case was difficult to see clearly. Or maybe she didn't want to get inside this particular murderer's head. "He's baiting me by leaving the note. I was part of the team hunting him. Maybe he's compelled to repeat last year since he failed."

"Do you know when the poinsettia was delivered?"

"Last night, around three in the morning. I have a doorbell camera, but all it caught was a shadowy figure dressed in black, and none of my neighbors saw anything."

Bennett picked up her cell phone and studied the photograph again. "The message on your door says the murders will begin again. That would indicate they haven't started yet."

Emilia froze. "The previous victims were held for a day or so before they were killed. Have any women gone missing recently?"

THREE

Half an hour later, Bennett pulled into the parking lot of the Fulton County Sheriff's Department. The two-story historical building also housed the courthouse. A large pine tree in front was decorated with ornaments and a wreath hung over the wooden front door. Plastic candy canes lined the walkway.

Emilia unsnapped her belt. "Do you think Sheriff Wilson will believe me?"

Bennett killed the engine. "It's no secret I wasn't fond of her predecessor, but Sheriff Wilson is a good cop. She'll take the threat seriously. More so if there is a missing woman that matches Derrick's type of victims."

They crossed the parking lot and entered the sheriff's department from the side door entrance. Holiday music filtered from a small radio at the front desk, but the deputy on duty was missing. Sheriff Wilson spotted them through the glass wall of her office. She waved them back. Bennett had called ahead of time and wasn't surprised to find Claire in the office on a Saturday afternoon. The sheriff often took the shift so her deputies could have the day off.

"Bennett, it's good to see you." Claire extended her hand for him to shake. Her blond hair was tucked into a bun at the nape of her neck and, even though it was the weekend, her uniform was perfectly ironed. Her gaze was sharp and direct. Only the freckles marching across her nose softened the tough appearance.

"Good to see you, Sheriff." Bennett shook her hand. "Thank you for meeting us on such short notice."

"It's not a problem." Claire turned to Emilia. "And you must be Special Agent Sanchez. I'm Sheriff Claire Wilson. Pleasure to meet you."

"Likewise." Emilia shook the sheriff's hand. "Please, call me Emilia."

"And you can call me Claire." She gestured to the chairs in front of her desk. "Have a seat. What can I help y'all with?"

Bennett explained about the threat left on Emilia's doorstep, along with the connection to Derrick Jackson and the murders. Claire listened carefully, interrupting only to ask clarifying questions. She scribbled notes on a pad.

When Bennett was finished, Claire studied the photograph on Emilia's phone. "Someone is clearly trying to scare you."

Emilia leaned forward. "I believe it's a warning, Sheriff. One we need to take seriously."

"I have every intention of doing so." Claire set the

phone down. "But I also don't want to make any assumptions. We don't have any evidence Derrick was working with someone else. Or that this threat is legitimate. There haven't been any murders in the county."

"What about missing women?"

"Nothing in the last few months."

Bennett breathed out. "Well, that's something to be grateful for."

"Agreed. I've reviewed the case files on the previous murders even though they happened before I was sheriff. There are holes. Most of the evidence collected from the cabin was never processed. Once Derrick died, my predecessor considered the case closed."

"Sheriff King relied on my ID." Emilia rubbed her forehead. "Which, based on this, was faulty."

"The ID was enough for an arrest, but not to close the case entirely. Victims—especially when drugged— often make mistakes." Claire met Emilia's gaze. "Understand, this is not your fault. The evidence from the cabin should have been processed and leads followed up on."

Bennett's esteem for the sheriff grew. Claire had sensed the weight of responsibility Emilia carried on her slender shoulders. But it wasn't her burden to bear.

Emilia's chin trembled. "Thank you, Claire."

Bennett patted Emilia's arm in solidarity before turning to Claire. "Sheriff, if you transfer the evidence you have to the state lab, I can put a rush on it."

Texas Rangers had priority at the state lab. Bennett had made the same offer to the previous sheriff, but he'd refused. Sheriff King kept an iron grip on his cases and rarely liked to share information or cooperate with other agencies. It'd caused a lot of friction between them.

Claire nodded. "Appreciate it. I'm not sure how much is in the storage room, since the case was closed. Some—or all—of the evidence may have been destroyed. I'll have a look as soon as we're done with this meeting."

"I'd like to review the case files as well," Bennett said. "I don't want to step on your toes here, Sheriff—"

"Not at all. As far as I'm concerned, Bennett, this is your case."

He breathed an internal sigh of relief. Bennett didn't need Claire's permission to investigate within the county since it was his jurisdiction, too, but it made things easier. "Thank you, Claire."

"I'm happy to work together. During the initial investigation, did you review any missing persons cases?"

Emilia leaned forward. "Sheriff, you read my mind. I was about to ask for access. I always suspected Derrick had killed more than the three women we knew about. The murders were too well-planned, too organized. Sheriff King rejected the notion and refused access to his missing persons files."

"I may have a new lead for you then." She rose from her chair and walked over to the filing cabinet. Claire removed a folder. "This case is seven years old, but it fits our pattern. Alice Nelson. Twenty-two. Disappeared one week before Christmas."

"Do you have a photograph?" Bennett asked.

Claire laid one on the desk. Bennett's heart sank. Alice was dark-haired and pretty with high cheekbones and a wide mouth. She fit right in with the other victims. "Who reported her missing?"

"Her mother. A deputy took Mrs. Nelson's statement, but the disappearance wasn't categorized as a high priority. Alice had a history of drug abuse and a habit of disappearing for days at a time."

Frustration flared, and Bennett battled it back. "They assumed she was on a bender and would reappear."

"Seems so." Claire scanned with a finger down the sheet. "Alice was a waitress at the Blue Grill. A deputy interviewed the night manager who confirmed Alice left at midnight when her shift was over. She caught a ride with a coworker, Derrick Jackson."

Emilia hit the desk with her hand. "This is information we needed during our previous investigation. Ooooo, I'm tempted to drive over to Sheriff King's house and give him a piece of my mind."

"You'll have to wait in line." Bennett resisted the urge to ball his hands into fists. Being angry with the previous sheriff wouldn't help them now. Better to focus on the matter at hand. "Did a deputy interview Derrick?"

Claire nodded. "Derrick confirmed he gave Alice a ride home but insisted he had nothing to do with her disappearance. After that, the case goes cold."

"Alice could be Derrick's first victim."

"That's a strong possibility," Claire said. "Since taking over as sheriff, I've gone through all the open case files for the last twenty years. Nothing else fits our pattern."

Emilia picked up Alice's photograph. "If Alice was

the first victim, working her case could lead us to Derrick's partner. Is Alice's mother still alive?"

"No. I attempted to contact her so we could take a fresh look at this case. Mrs. Nelson died six months after her daughter disappeared. Heart attack. However, Alice has a grandmother who still lives in town. Marcy Nelson. I haven't spoken to her yet." Claire held up a finger before searching through the file. "There was also a note about Alice's boyfriend. Hold on...Yes, here it is. John McInnis. It looks like a deputy was supposed to interview him but never did."

"John McInnis. I know that name." Emilia's brow crinkled. "Where do I know that name from?"

"John manages rental properties. Chances are you've seen his signs around town." Bennett rocked back on his heels. "John may have some insight into the case. It's worth talking to him."

Claire tilted her head. "If Alice is the first victim, why would the killers wait so long before striking again? There are seven years between her murder and the next one."

"Maybe not," Emilia said. "Call the surrounding counties and ask them to search their missing persons records. Specifically, we're looking for dark-haired single women who went missing during the holidays. Derrick and his partner may have selected victims from outside Fulton County during those seven years. It would make connecting the cases harder."

Bennett's gut clenched. His gaze shot to the photograph of Alice. Was Emilia right? Were there more victims? If so, it meant the killer was far more deadly, far more proficient, than they'd realized.

And he was still out there.

McInnis Management was located in the center of town. Originally a home from the 1930s, it'd been converted into an office space. Emilia's heels thumped against the wooden front porch, and then she paused to read the sign on the door. It instructed guests to let themselves in. The door handle was frigid against her bare palm.

An empty desk sat in the entrance. Two love seats and a coffee table served as a seating area. Bennett shut the door behind them. Beyond the glass, the sky was getting dark as thunderclouds rolled in.

Emilia tugged on the scarf around her neck. "Hello? Anyone here?"

Footsteps came from an office in the back. Moments later, a man appeared. John McInnis. Emilia recognized him from his driver's license photo. John was tall and good-looking with a trim beard and striking blue eyes. The sleeves on his button-down shirt were rolled up to the elbows.

When he saw Emilia, a flash of something akin to recognition crossed his face before he smoothed out his expression. "Hi, welcome to McInnis Management. I'm John. How can I help you?"

He was pretending to not know her. An alarm bell

dinged internally, but Emilia decided to play the game and see where it went.

"Mr. McInnis, my name is Special Agent Emilia Sanchez." She flashed her credentials before gesturing to Bennett. "And this Texas Ranger Bennett Knox. We'd like to speak with you about a case we're investigating. Is there someplace we can sit down?"

"Sure. Come on back to my office." He waved for them to follow. "Special Agent? Are you with the FBI?"

"No, sir, state police."

Emilia and Bennett followed John to the inner office. Files were spread across the conference table. The desk contained neat stacks of paper and a half-drunk mug of coffee. John gestured to two chairs across from the desk. "Please sit. And ignore the mess. We're working on an annual assessment of our properties."

"Annual assessment?"

"Yes, we tour the homes and apartment complexes to make sure there aren't any maintenance problems." John settled in the leather chair behind his desk and flashed a charming smile. "But you didn't come here to discuss the woes of property management. You mentioned a case you're investigating. What case?"

Bennett set his cowboy hat on the desk along with an umbrella. "We're following up on Alice Nelson disappearance."

John's brows lifted to his hairline. "Alice Nelson? I thought that case was closed."

"Who told you that?"

"N-n-no one. I just..." He ran a hand over his face

and took a deep breath. A flush colored his cheeks. "Forgive me, I'm shocked. Alice disappeared a long time ago after accepting a ride home from Derrick Jackson. After he was found guilty of murdering those other women, I just assumed..."

"No, Mr. McInnis, the case is still active." Bennett removed a pad from his shirt pocket, along with a pen. "Did you know Derrick Jackson?"

John shifted in his seat. "Not well. Derrick was one of the maintenance men for our properties." His gaze darted between Emilia and Bennett. "Of course, that's not something we would like to have advertised again. It took forever for things to die down after last year. It was terrible for our business—"

"No, sir," Bennett said. "We'll keep it quiet."

"Thank you." His shoulders dropped. "We do background checks on everyone who works for us. Derrick didn't have a criminal record. When I heard about what he'd done, I was horrified. One of the victims—Rachel McAdams—lived on one of our properties. I always wondered if Derrick saw her while doing maintenance work. It's awful to think about."

Emilia sat up straight. Derrick wasn't the only one connected to Rachel. John was, too, since she was living in a property he managed. "Did you know Rachel McAdams?"

The young woman had been the serial killer's final victim last year. While returning home from work, Rachel was grabbed from the parking lot of her apartment complex. She was killed and left in a nearby park one week before Christmas.

John shook his head. "Not personally. We have managers that handle the day-to-day business at the apartment complexes. But when I saw in the media that Derrick was responsible for those other women's deaths, I assumed Alice had been one of his victims."

Emilia leaned forward. "Did you ever speak to the sheriff about your theory regarding Alice's disappearance?"

"No. Why? Should I have?"

She found it strange. If John believed Derrick was involved in Alice's disappearance, why not speak to the sheriff? Alice's case had never been connected to the others. Then again, even in small towns, people minded their own business from time to time. And Sheriff King never took kindly to interference in his cases.

Emilia needed to be careful. She was personally involved in the investigation and it might cause her to see things that weren't actually there.

"How well did you know Alice?" she asked.

"Not well. We went on a few dates, but the relationship wasn't serious. I considered us friends though."

"You were identified as Alice's boyfriend in the case file."

"No. It was probably Alice's mom who said that. I met her once when I picked Alice up for a date. Mrs. Nelson believed we were a couple, and I didn't correct her." He shrugged. "Silly, perhaps, but the assumption seemed harmless. I didn't want to upset Mrs. Nelson or embarrass Alice."

The explanation was reasonable, but something about the man put Emilia on edge. She couldn't put her finger on why. His answers were too smooth, as if they'd been practiced.

"Did Alice discuss any problems before her disappearance?" Bennett asked. "Or complain about someone bothering her?"

"Not that I know of." John was quiet for a long moment. He tugged on his shirt. "Listen, I don't want to speak badly about Alice, but she didn't have the best taste in friends. It was part of the reason I hesitated to move past a few dates with her. Alice hung out in a crowd that liked to party."

"Drugs?"

He nodded. "And alcohol. I had just taken over the business after my father's death and I didn't have time for all that nonsense." John blew out a breath. "Alice was a sweet girl, and smart. But there was a self-destructive side to her. Her mother and father had a terrible divorce, and it really messed her up."

Emilia felt a pang of sympathy for Alice. She knew what it was like to feel lost. "Did you speak or see Alice on the night she disappeared?"

"Yes. I stopped by the Blue Grill on my way home to pick up a to-go order, and Alice was working the register. We chatted about our families and work. Alice mentioned she was catching a ride home from Derrick. He worked in the back as a dishwasher."

"What kind of relationship did Derrick and Alice have?"

"They were friendly. I know they hung out sometimes. Beyond that, I couldn't say." He checked his watch and rose. "I'm so sorry, but I need to get back to work. I was supposed to have these property assessments organized last month, and it didn't happen."

"Absolutely." Emilia rose. "Thank you for your time."

She offered her hand. John took it, clasping her hand in both of his. "It was a pleasure to meet you, Special Agent Sanchez."

A shiver raced down her spine. John's expression was perfectly polite, but something lurked in the shadows of his eyes. Emilia yanked her hand back.

Was she staring at a killer?

Cold wind slapped Bennett's cheeks as he left John's office. Dusk had given way to evening and rain pattered against the small porch. Emilia's expression was taut as she shrugged on her jacket.

Bennett settled his hat on his head before unfurling his umbrella and offering it to her. "Here."

"No, we can share." She slid closer to him. "The car isn't far."

His heart skipped a beat. There was no chance of a romantic relationship with Emilia, but it was hard to ignore the effect she had on him.

Bennett tilted the umbrella so it covered Emilia more

than him. The scent of her perfume teased his nose. It was clean and fresh, like citrus. He placed his hand on the small of her back and guided her down the sidewalk.

Emilia kept her voice low. "What did you think of John?"

"He seemed helpful and answered our questions. Still, I want to look into him more. He's connected to several of the victims and Derrick."

She nodded. "John pretended not to know me, but I swear he recognized me when we walked in."

"He may remember you from last year. Your face was on the news for a few nights in a row."

She frowned. "Maybe. I'm close to this case and that colors my reactions." Emilia hopped into the passenger seat. "Let's visit Mrs. Nelson and see what she can tell us."

Marcy Nelson lived two minutes away on a residential street close to the center of town. Her home was small, but the yard was tidy. Bennett handed Emilia his extra umbrella, and they got out of the car.

Water spattered Bennett's boots as he traversed the walkway to the front door. He pushed the doorbell, but no one answered. The window curtains were drawn.

"I don't think she's home," Emilia said.

"Yoo-hoo!" A neighbor waved from across the street. Bennett recognized her as one of his mother's friends, Jan Kirkland. He waved back.

Jan wrapped her sweater around her waist, hugging herself against the cold. "Bennett, are you looking for Mrs. Nelson?"

"Yes, ma'am, we are."

"She's on a trip visiting her sister and won't be back till Tuesday. Is everything okay?"

"Perfectly fine, Mrs. Kirkland." Bennett crossed the street and jogged up to the other woman's porch. "Do you have a phone number for Mrs. Nelson?"

"I'm afraid I don't. She doesn't use a cell phone and her sister recently moved. I don't have the new number. Marcy may call and check in with me though."

He handed Jan one of his cards. "If she does, would you have her call me? It's important."

She accepted the card. "Of course. And please tell your mother the quilting circle meeting moved to Wednesday night, if you don't mind. I have half a dozen other ladies to phone. It would save me a call."

"Absolutely."

He flashed Jan a smile before heading back to the truck. Emilia was already in the passenger seat. Bennett got in and started the engine. He flipped the heat on high to ward off the chill before pulling away from the curb.

"What's the game plan now, Emilia? This case isn't going to wrap up tonight, and I don't feel comfortable with you heading back home unprotected."

"Actually, I don't need to. I never unpacked from my trip to El Paso, so I have a suitcase of clothes in my car. I just need a laundry mat and a hotel."

"You don't need a hotel. You can stay on the ranch."

"That's a kind offer, Bennett, but I don't want to put your family at risk—"

He raised a hand. "The ranch has a first-rate security

system. It's the safest place for you, Emilia." Bennett flashed her a half-grin. "Besides, if you stay in a hotel, then I'll have to keep watch over you by sleeping outside in my truck. Save this old man from a backache and agree to stay on the ranch."

She laughed and lightly smacked him on the arm. "You aren't old."

"Tell that to my back."

"Okay, okay. You win." Emilia smiled. "I'll stay on the ranch."

"Good decision." Bennett turned onto the country road toward home. His windshield wipers swiped at the rain. "Fair warning, my mom will convince you to help with Christmas decorating. Make sure you're ready for a lot of holiday cheer. It's—"

Glass shattered. Something whizzed past Bennett and thudded into the dash.

A bullet.

His heart jumped as his gaze shot to the side-view mirror. A large vehicle, driving without its lights on, was tailing them. Cold air rushed in through the destroyed rear window. It was too dark to make out the license plate. Another bullet slammed into Bennett's truck.

Bennett swerved and hit the gas. "Get down, Emilia!"

She bent at the waist. Out of the corner of his eye, Bennett saw Emilia grab the radio to call in their location to dispatch. Smart woman. It allowed Bennett to focus on driving. He dodged and weaved, attempting to put some distance between them and the shooter. Rain made the road slick, and his tires hydroplaned. Bennett gripped the wheel, struggling to maintain control before they careened into the ditch. Prayers slid from his lips.

A roar came from behind them as the shooter got closer. Bullets pinged off the vehicle and more glass shattered.

Emilia cried out.

FOUR

Bennett paced the length of the emergency room. Emilia was inside being examined by the doctor. A bullet had grazed her arm, and the wound probably needed stitches.

Tonight had been a close call. Too close. Bennett mentally berated himself for letting down his guard, even for a moment. Emilia was his Achilles heel. He liked being with her. He'd missed her friendship, and while chatting on the way home, it'd been like old times when their conversation was light and easy. But that was no excuse. He had one responsibility: keeping Emilia safe.

Bennett didn't have a personal life. No wife. No children. His job as a Texas Ranger was everything. If he failed...he didn't have anything left.

Mistakes like tonight couldn't happen again.

His cell phone buzzed and Bennett pulled it from his pocket. The name flashing across his screen was a familiar one. Randy King, the former sheriff. Bennett answered.

"What's this I hear about you causing a ruckus?" Randy's voice boomed over the line. Bennett envisioned the sheriff leaning back in his chair, a cigarette hanging from the corner of his mouth. "I leave town for two weeks to visit my wife's family for Thanksgiving, and you're digging into old cases and questioning folks."

Bennett wasn't surprised to hear from Randy. The former sheriff was retired, but he kept his finger on the pulse of the town. His thirty-plus year career in Fulton County had left its mark, and everyone, including Bennett, still called him Sheriff King.

Bennett explained about the threat against Emilia and being shot at. "We believe it's connected to Derrick Jackson. Emilia isn't sure Derrick was the only one in the cabin with them. Do you know of anyone Derrick might've been working with?"

Randy was quiet for so long, Bennett thought the connection had dropped. "Sheriff?"

"I'm here. There were no other fingerprints found in Derrick's cabin. We questioned the neighbors, and no one mentioned another vehicle. I believe you're barking up the wrong tree, son. I'm sure Emilia has enemies. Have you looked into the criminals she's helped put away?"

"There are investigators working on that." Bennett lowered his voice as a nurse passed by. "What do you remember about Alice Nelson's disappearance?"

"Nelson? That girl ran off with her boyfriend. Hold on...I'll remember his name."

Bennett fought back a sharp reply. Randy wouldn't

have to remember the boyfriend's name if it was written in the case file. It was one of the many things they'd butted heads about. Randy had never been particular about following procedure.

Randy blew out a breath. "I can't remember right this moment, but it'll come to me. I'll text you. Why are you asking about Alice Nelson, anyway?"

"Because Derrick Jackson gave her a ride home from work. According to the case file, he was the last person to see her alive."

"Nope, that ain't right. There was a party that night and Alice was there. When I get home, I'll dig around and find my personal notes."

"Didn't you turn your personal notes over when you retired?"

"I'm organizing them. Ain't no need to rush me, son."

The doors to the emergency room swished open. Claire marched in. The sheriff spotted Bennett and headed in his direction.

Bennett said a quick goodbye to Sheriff King and tucked the phone back in his pocket before turning to Claire. "Word of warning, Randy King will call you by the end of the evening."

"Too late. He's already left five messages with my front desk." She frowned. "Someone in my department is feeding him information, but I don't know who."

"I'm sure it's several people. Not to mention the townsfolk. There isn't much that stays secret in Fulton."

She muttered a reply he didn't hear before planting her hands on her hips. "What happened tonight?"

He provided a rundown of the shooting. Claire jotted a couple of things down on a notepad. "Can you give me a description of the vehicle?"

"No. It was dark and raining. I can't even tell you if the vehicle was a truck or an SUV."

"Well, I looked at your vehicle in the parking lot. I think Emilia was struck by accident. Most of the bullets were directed at the driver's side."

Bennett had been in such a rush to get Emilia inside the emergency room, he hadn't taken the time to study his vehicle. His gaze narrowed. "The shooter was aiming for me. Why? To force me off the road so he could kidnap Emilia?"

"A definite possibility. Anyone set on killing the pair of you would've fired at both sides of the vehicle." She paused. "Of course, we have to consider this attack may not be connected to the threat against Emilia. You may have been the primary target."

"Doubtful. I have my fair share of enemies, but this is too much of a coincidence."

"What if both are true? Think about it this way, Bennett. You rescued Emilia from the woods before the killer found her. You took her from him, so to speak. He might want revenge."

Bennett hadn't considered that angle, but it had merit. He didn't care about the risk to himself. Being a Texas Ranger was dangerous, even under normal circumstances, and he'd accepted that a long time ago. But he wouldn't let anyone harm Emilia. Not while there was breath in his body.

He crossed his arms over his chest, keeping his eye on the closed exam room door. "This has to be connected to the murders from last year, but we need proof."

"Agreed. What did you find out from John McInnis?"

Bennett ran through the conversation with the businessman. "John has a connection to several of the victims and Derrick. He's worth looking into more. Were you able to search the evidence room?"

Claire's mouth flattened. "Everything in connection to the murders and Emilia's abduction has been destroyed. Probably done in the ordinary course of business since the case was officially closed. The only thing we have are the case files, and they're incomplete. Sheriff King liked to exert control over his cases and did so by keeping his deputies in the dark about evidence and interviews. It's a terrible way to run a department."

"You won't hear any argument from me on that point." Bennett rubbed the back of his neck, fighting his exhaustion and frustration. "So right now, the best lead we have are the bullets embedded in my truck."

"Yep. If we're lucky, the killer used that gun in a prior crime. I'll have the vehicle towed to the evidence shed."

"Thanks." Bennett would have to use his personal vehicle for the next few days. "Keep me updated on what you find out."

"Will do." She tucked the notepad and pen into her pocket. "Stay safe in the meantime, Bennett. Whoever is behind this isn't playing around. He failed tonight, and that's liable to make him angry. I'm worried about what he'll do next."

"So am I, Claire. So am I."

Emilia winced as the doctor secured the bandage to her arm. The wound hadn't needed stitches, but it was deep enough to be painful. She would be sore tomorrow.

The doctor's gaze shifted from the bandage to the scar streaking down her forearm. Heat flooded Emilia's cheeks, and she braced herself for questions, but the doctor merely stepped back. Emilia breathed a sigh of relief. It was silly. The scars were nothing to be ashamed of, but she hated them all the same.

The doctor collected a tablet and electronic pen from the counter. "Change the dressing tomorrow and follow up with your regular physician if you run a fever. Someone will be in momentarily with your discharge papers."

"Thanks. Could you send in the Texas Ranger standing outside the door?"

"Sure thing."

The doctor left. The sound of voices filtered into the room. Emilia tugged on the sleeve of her sweater, covering the bandage and her scars seconds before Bennett walked in. His hair was mussed as if he'd been running his hands through it and worry clouded his eyes.

"How many stitches?" Bennett asked.

Emilia hopped off the exam table. "No stitches, just some butterfly closures. We didn't have to come to the emergency room after all." She flashed him a smile and winked. "A stop by the pharmacy would've done the job."

He rolled his eyes. "Your arm would fall off and you'd call it a flesh wound and ask to drive by the pharmacy."

She laughed. His comment wasn't far from the truth.

Bennett's expression grew serious. "Emilia, I'm sorry. I should've been paying better attention—"

"Don't even start down that road, Bennett Knox. You saved my life tonight. If anyone should apologize in this situation, it's me." Emilia placed a hand on his arm. His shirt was soft under her palm and the warmth of his skin seeped through the fabric. "I'm sorry for my behavior over the last year. After Derrick's attack, I just wanted to move on with my life. I blocked out anything that reminded me of what happened and our friendship got caught up in the mess. It was wrong."

"There's no rule book for how you're supposed to behave after escaping from a deranged serial killer." Bennett locked eyes with her, his expression sympathetic. "I never blamed you, Emilia. And I always considered us friends."

A sense of relief washed over Emilia. Her apology to Bennett was long overdue and having his forgiveness and understanding lifted a weight from her shoulders. She gave into the urge to step forward and hug him. "Thank you, Bennett."

He hugged her back. Bennett's embrace was gentle and comforting. It struck Emilia how safe she felt within the circle of his arms. She laid her head on his strong chest. The warm scent of his cologne and the sound of his heartbeat under her ear soothed her tattered emotions.

A knock came on the exam room door, breaking the moment. Emilia slipped from Bennett's arms. "Come in."

A man in scrubs entered. His blond hair was slicked back from his face and he carried a clipboard. "Okay, Ms. Sanchez, I have your discharge..." His mouth dropped open. "Emilia?"

Emilia studied the man's face. He was in his thirties with the trim figure of a swimmer. His nose was crooked, as if it'd been broken a time or two, and a faint scar crossed the corner of his mouth. Nothing about him seemed familiar.

"I'm sorry, have we met?" she asked.

"It was a long time ago." He smiled, flashing uneven teeth. "Henry Stillman."

The name rang a distinct bell in her mind, but Emilia still couldn't place him. Confusion must have shown in her expression because Henry added, "We lived in the same foster home." His gaze drifted to the ceiling. "Uh, what was the foster mother's name? Mrs. Berry. No, that's not it..."

She sucked in a breath as the memory surfaced. "Mrs. Appleton. Linda Appleton."

He snapped his fingers. "That's it. She was one of the good ones. Remember she ran a bakery so whenever we came home from school there were fresh pastries on the table. Muffins and scones. Sometimes cookies. I used to take more than my fair share and hide them under the bed."

She remembered. Henry had been a thin, scrappy teenager with a chip on his shoulder. They hadn't lived together very long. Emilia left that foster home to live with her mother, who'd completed rehab. Within six months, her mom was using again.

Henry's gaze drifted to Bennett. The ranger stepped forward, offering his hand. "Texas Ranger Bennett Knox."

"Nice to meet you." Henry shook Bennett's hand and then turned back to Emilia. "So how have you been?"

"Good, thanks." She smiled, but it felt strained at the edges. Henry hadn't been kind to her in the foster home. Quite the opposite, in fact. He'd been a bully.

Henry shook his head. "Man, it's been ages since I thought about Mrs. Appleton. I left her home shortly after you did. Bounced around here and there until I aged out of the system. The state paid for college so I decided on nursing. Moved back here afterward. My dad lives in town. He got sober and we've patched things up so I have family nearby."

"That's good." Emilia cocked her head. "I'm surprised you recognized me, Henry. It's been a long time."

"I have a memory for faces. I saw your name on the discharge paperwork, but it wasn't until I saw you that I made the connection." He frowned. "I overheard the doctor say you'd been shot. Are you okay?"

"I'm fine."

Henry edged closer. "What happened?"

His curiosity irked her. Henry had set fire to her

homework, snuck into the bathroom while she was taking a shower to steal her clothes, and lied about her to their foster mother. He'd tormented Emilia. She had never considered them friends.

Emilia gestured to the clipboard. "Is that the discharge paperwork?"

"Oh, yeah." Henry laughed. "Sorry. I'm sure you want to get out of here."

She took a deep breath and reminded herself to give grace. It'd been almost two decades since she'd seen Henry last. Although she didn't have fond memories of him, Henry seemed nice enough now. People changed. Lord knows, she had. Being polite cost her nothing.

Emilia signed the paperwork quickly and collected her coat. "Thanks, Henry."

"No problem. Hey, listen, give me your number. We can have coffee sometime and catch up."

She hugged her coat tighter. "I'm only in town for work, Henry. But thanks for the offer. Take care."

Emilia hurried from the room.

Bennett caught up with her in the hall. "Everything okay?"

"Fine." She rolled her shoulders and the bandage on her arm tugged at the skin. "I didn't like Henry when we were kids. It's a long story." Her steps slowed. "Where are we going, by the way? Is your truck drivable?"

"No. It's being towed to the evidence shed. My dad is in the waiting room. He'll give us a lift home."

"Bennett, considering the shooting, it's not a good idea for me to stay on the ranch with your family. I'm perfectly capable of protecting myself. I'm a trained police officer."

"You are capable. There's no question about that." He met her gaze. "But it's foolish to refuse my help, Emilia. Please don't. The ranch is safe, otherwise I wouldn't have suggested staying there. Trust me."

Bennett breathed a sigh of relief as the gates of One Horse Ranch swung open. He'd kept watch during the car ride from the hospital, and there'd been no sign of trouble. Still it was good to be home.

The property had been in Bennett's family for six generations. The main house sat on a slight incline. Made of wood and stone, it sported a wraparound porch complete with rocking chairs. Christmas lights twinkled from every available surface including windows, rooftop, and the bushes. An inflatable Santa danced next to some plastic reindeer. Spotlight focused on the large nativity scene next to the walkway leading to the front door.

Emilia gasped from the back seat. "The house looks so pretty."

"Yeah. Y'all were busy today." Bennett chuckled. "I hate to see the electricity bill next month."

His father, Zeke, snorted. "There's no stopping your mother at Christmastime. You know that. She had me on the roof adding lights until the sun went down. I'm still not done. There are five more packages."

Exasperation laced Zeke's tone, but it was for show.

Bennett's father was burly and gruff, but he had a soft spot as big as the Rio Grande for Joanna Knox. Zeke would move heaven and earth to make his wife happy. Kids, too, come to think of it.

The front door to the house opened before they'd even parked the truck. Bennett's mother appeared in the doorway, wiping her hands on the apron tied around her waist. The Christmas lights flickered across her wide smile.

Bennett exited the truck and opened the rear door for Emilia. She climbed out. "I have to grab my overnight bag from my car."

"I'll get it," Bennett said. "Just pop the trunk and head inside. It's cold."

Emilia hit a button on the fob and the trunk swung open. Bennett removed the small suitcase.

On the porch, his mother embraced Emilia. The murmur of their voices drifted across the driveway, but not the actual words. Joanna patted Emilia's cheek and ushered her inside.

Bennett smiled. His mother had a fondness for Emilia. Both his parents did.

Bennett carried the suitcase up the walkway. His father waited at the bottom of the porch steps. "What kind of trouble are we dealing with, son?"

"I'm not sure. Emilia's in danger. That much is certain. She's received a threat connected to the Derrick Jackson murders. He may not have been working alone. Or someone wants us to believe he wasn't."

Zeke's expression tightened. His hands went to his

hips where the butt of his handgun was visible underneath his jacket. Bennett's father never left the house without his weapon. He had a concealed carry license and was a crack shot.

His gaze swept across the yard. "I'll go down to the foreman house and talk to Grayson. Let him know what's going on so he can keep watch."

Grayson had spent five years in the army, and Bennett had no concerns about his brother-in-law's ability to guard the ranch.

"Do you want me to go with you?" Bennett asked.

"No, son. You stick close to Emilia. That woman has been through a lot, more than her fair share." Zeke clapped Bennett on the shoulder. "I'm glad you brought her here. We'll keep her safe."

Bennett had expected nothing less from his father, but it was still nice to hear the words out loud. "Thanks, Dad."

Zeke nodded and headed across the grass to the foreman house.

Bennett went inside the house and set Emilia's bag by the door. The warm scents of tomato sauce and oregano greeted him. Voices filtered from the kitchen. Bennett followed them and discovered his mother and Emilia in the kitchen.

Joanna greeted him with a wide smile, although worry lingered in her eyes. His mother would never say anything, but Bennett knew she fretted about his job. Being shot at today hadn't helped allay those concerns.

"Hey, Mom." Bennett scooped her up for a big hug

and kissed her cheek. "Love the decorations. Real sorry I missed helping to put them up."

She chuckled and swatted his arm. "Don't lie to your mother. Are you hungry?"

"Starved. Please tell me that amazing scent is Nana's famous spaghetti."

"You're in luck because it is. There's apple crumble for dessert too." Joanna waved toward Emilia who was filling glasses with iced tea. "We were just setting the table for dinner. Soon as your dad comes back, we can eat."

Bennett quickly washed his hands and then pitched in to set the table. He teased his mother and Emilia, keeping the conversation light. The two women joined in the fun.

By the time dinner was ready, the tension had eased from Emilia's shoulders. She laughed at a story his mom was telling, her eyes lighting up with joy. Bennett's breath caught and his heart quickened.

Emilia was gorgeous, but more than that, she was brave. Maybe too brave. She'd carried the weight of Derrick's attack around for the last year, and now her life was being threatened again. Bennett couldn't control everything, but he could ease the burden from her shoulders. Protect her. Be her friend.

Bennett vowed to keep Emilia safe, no matter the cost. Even if it meant his life.

He prayed it wouldn't come to that.

FIVE

Emilia sat up, clenched fists raised, a scream bubbling in her throat. Her pulse beat rapid-fire.

She blinked. The woods and the man holding the knife faded as the bedroom came into focus. Morning sunlight filtered through the pretty blue curtains. It smelled of vanilla and wood polish. Emilia wasn't in danger. She was at Bennett's ranch, in the guest bedroom.

Emilia sucked in a ragged breath. Her pajama top was soaked with sweat. She hadn't had a nightmare like that in months. It'd been so vivid and real. She kicked back the covers and papers slid from the bed. Police reports from last year's murders. She'd fallen asleep reading them, searching for any clue that could lead them to Derrick's partner. Was it any wonder she'd had nightmares?

If only she could remember the killer's face or some

distinguishing mark. But most of her captivity was a blur. She couldn't even recall escaping the cabin.

Emilia collected the papers and stuffed them back into the folder before heading into the bathroom. Fifteen minutes and a shower later, her heart rate was back to normal. It was Sunday, which meant church. Bennett's family attended the one in town and Emilia was happy to visit again. Prayer and an uplifting service was exactly what she needed. She dressed in slacks and a thick cable sweater. Emilia made sure the sleeve was adjusted at her wrist to cover the scars on her arm before heading downstairs.

The scent of coffee pulled Emilia to the kitchen. Bennett's mom, Joanna, stood at the island reading a magazine. Her gray hair was cut in a pixie style that suited her perfect cheekbones and large green eyes. Holiday music filtered softly from the radio.

Joanna smiled. "Morning, dear. Would you like some coffee? Or I can make tea, if you prefer?"

"No, coffee is fine. I can get it." Emilia selected a cup from the wooden mug rack on the wall. The coffee was strong and dark with subtle hints of nutmeg. "Is this a special blend? It smells wonderful."

"I love it too. It's a limited edition for the holidays." Joanna opened the fridge and pulled out caramel creamer. "I remembered how much you liked this and picked some up at the store yesterday."

Warmth flooded through Emilia's chest at the other woman's kindness. "Thank you."

She added a generous amount to her cup. Had

anyone ever bought her favorite creamer? Had anyone—other than Bennett or his mom—even remembered how she liked her coffee? The answer was simple. No. Emilia wasn't used to being taken care of. Her own parents had been a whirlwind of dysfunction. Foster care had been little better. Survival had required complete independence, but it came at a cost. Being around Bennett's family again made her realize how lonely her life was.

Joanna removed a mixing bowl from the cabinet. "If you give me twenty minutes, I'll have a batch of blueberry pancakes whipped up before we head to church."

Emilia put out a hand to stop her. "Please don't go to any trouble on my account."

"I'm not, hon. Bennett hasn't had breakfast yet either, and my granddaughter will run through this house in half an hour searching for something to eat."

"Oh, well, can I help?"

Joanna opened the pantry and started pulling out ingredients. "Why don't you take Bennett a cup of coffee? He's down at the barn in his office." She winked. "Between you and me, my son can be a real bear if he doesn't get two cups in the morning."

Emilia laughed. She couldn't imagine Bennett grouchy. The man was easygoing, and although she'd seen him under tense circumstances while working a murder investigation, he'd never raised his voice.

She poured a cup for Bennett, topped off her own, and then headed outside. Grass crunched under her boots. The cold air stung her cheeks and her breath puffed out in front of her. In the distance, horses grazed.

Inside the barn, Bennett's dog raced to meet her. Duke's tail wagged, but Emilia couldn't pet him because she was holding the coffees. "Hey, buddy."

Bennett came out of a back room, dressed in well-worn jeans and cowboy boots. He was handsome enough to grace the cover of a magazine. Or a romance novel. Emilia's heart skipped a beat before taking off at a gallop.

"Morning." Bennett smiled, his green eyes lighting up with warmth at the sight of her.

Emilia's cheeks heated and butterflies rioted in her stomach. Her attraction to Bennett had been easier to ignore from hundreds of miles away. Up close, it was impossible to deny. But there was nowhere for these feelings to go. Bennett's life was here, on this ranch, with his family. Emilia had the strength to handle being in Fulton County in doses, but every day? That wasn't possible. Her nightmare was proof enough.

"Good morning." Emilia thrust one of the coffee mugs toward Bennett. "Here, this is for you. Your mom swears you're grouchy without it, and we can't have that."

He rolled his eyes. "Don't believe a word my mom says."

"Anything new on the case?" Emilia scratched Duke behind the ears. His tail thumped against the floor.

"As a matter of fact, yes." Bennett sipped his coffee and then waved her back. "Come into the office. I have something to show you."

The office had stained-wood walls and a sealed-concrete floor. A desk sat facing a large window overlooking the pasture.

Emilia ran her hand over a bull riding trophy. Bennett's name was engraved along the edge. "I didn't know you were a bull rider."

"Only for a bit while in college." He flashed a heart-stopping smile. "Then I traded my spurs for a lawman's badge. Mom was disappointed. She hoped I would pick a less adventurous career."

"Considering we were shot at last night, I can't say I blame her."

The mirth left his expression as Bennett gestured to a whiteboard running along the far wall. "This is what I wanted to show you. Claire heard from the surrounding counties. Ten additional women meet our parameters. All of them are active missing person cases."

Emilia's hand tightened around her coffee mug. Photos of the women were hung on the whiteboard with magnets. Dates were underneath each picture, indicating when they'd disappeared. Bennett had also added Alice's photo, along with the three victims attributed to Derrick.

Fourteen women in total. It made her heart ache. *Why, God? Why?*

"Most of the cases weren't investigated thoroughly because the women engaged in high-risk behaviors," Bennett continued. "Drug use, abusive boyfriends, home-less, etc."

"That would make it easier for police to believe they had simply run off. Like Alice." She tapped the young woman's photograph. "She's still the first victim."

Bennett nodded. "So far, yes."

"None of the women's bodies have been recovered."

Emilia scanned the board, thinking out loud. "That means the killer—or killers—have a graveyard somewhere. Or they dumped the bodies in the woods, deep enough they haven't been discovered yet. What happened to the land and the cabin Derrick owned after his death?"

The cabin she'd been held in. Nearly killed in. All the missing women—including Alice—could be buried in the vicinity.

Bennett frowned. "I was curious about that myself and looked it up this morning. The land was bought by a corporation, Ignite Development. They own several parcels around the lake including the one next to Derrick's property."

"Who owns the corporation?"

"No idea. It's based out of Delaware. That state allows the owners to be anonymous. However, the attorney listed as a point of contact is Sheriff King's son, Malcolm."

Emilia arched her brows. "Small world."

"Malcolm's a friend of mine. He handles most of the civil work in the county. Buying and selling property, business investments, probate. His dad and I have had our differences, but Malcolm's different. He's a good guy and an excellent lawyer."

"We should make a formal request for access to the property so we can search it using cadaver dogs. I doubt we'll get it, since Ignite is probably owned by Derrick's partner. He used the corporation to hide his identity.

Still, it's worth a shot. I guarantee those missing women are buried on that land."

Emilia had almost been one of the victims. Her mind flashed back to the nightmare. Running through the woods, being chased, the fear so thick it choked her.

Bennett placed a hand on her arm. His palm was warm, even through the thick fabric of her sweater. It jolted Emilia from the dark train of her thoughts.

He dipped his head down to meet her eyes. "You okay?"

"I'm fine."

She gave herself a mental shake. She'd survived Derrick's attack. Now these women needed Emilia to be their voice.

She wouldn't rest until justice was served.

Bennett hadn't planned on discussing the case before church, but Emilia asked. He wouldn't lie to her. She'd had enough people in her life let her down and hurt her, starting with her parents. Bennett refused to be one more. Still, the dusky shadows under her gorgeous eyes bothered him. She hadn't slept well.

Emilia stepped to the whiteboard and tapped Alice's photograph. "We made mistakes last year. I want to make sure we get it right this time."

The mistakes hadn't been theirs. Sheriff King had denied them access to important case files and ignored their advice. But Bennett understood what she meant.

This time, they wouldn't stop working until there were answers.

She turned to face him. "I reviewed the case files from the last three murders. Nothing in them helps identify Derrick's partner."

Bennett leaned against the desk. "Walk me through it, Emilia. I know serial killers can form partnerships, but I've never come across it personally in my career. Until now."

"Generally, there is a dominant partner and a subservient one. Each of them gets something from the other. The dominant partner gets complete loyalty from the subservient one. The subservient receives love or attention."

"Which was Derrick?"

"Based on what I know so far, subservient. Derrick was unorganized. He didn't graduate from high school and had a history of drug abuse. I didn't think he could commit these crimes. They were too well-planned and, frankly, he didn't seem smart enough to carry them out."

Bennett had thought the same. Until Emilia identified him as her attacker.

She crossed her arms over her midsection. "I remember thinking when he approached me in the parking lot that he was harmless. Derrick said he had information about the crimes I needed to hear." She shook her head. "In the hospital, I felt so stupid for allowing myself to be fooled. Anyone can be a killer and profiling isn't an exact science."

"Except, it seems, you weren't entirely wrong."

Bennett pushed off from the desk. "Let's assume we have two killers working together and that Derrick is the subservient one. Derrick had a history of drug abuse." He waved a finger at the women on the whiteboard. "Most of these missing women did too."

Her eyes widened. "Derrick knew them. He was the scout, searching for potential victims based on certain parameters. Dark-haired. Pretty. Single. Once Derrick identifies a woman, he would confer with his partner, who makes the final decision."

"Then Derrick grabs the woman, either through deception or by snatching them."

"Right. Alice got in his car willingly for a ride home. I was—along with the other victims from last year—kidnapped." She paced the room. "Derrick delivers the woman to his partner. The dominant one is the killer. He's controlled. Patient. Everything is about him. The victim they choose, the poinsettia left with the bodies, killing during the holiday season. They have meaning for Derrick's partner, not Derrick."

"It explains so much. Your profile wasn't wrong, Emilia. We didn't have all the pieces." Bennett moved down to the end of the board. "What I can't understand is why they broke the pattern? All the other women are still missing—maybe dumped in the woods, as you pointed out. But Derrick and his partner drop these final three off in public parks."

"Escalation. It wasn't enough to kidnap women and kill them. Derrick's partner wanted more. Placing his victims in a public place gives him a prolonged power rush. The news reports would've fed his ego. When the police don't catch him, he becomes invincible. He keeps upping the risk. Ultimately, he had Derrick kidnap me."

"And the message left on your doorstep?"

"The killer failed last year because I escaped. That would've been a blow to his ego. He's compelled to finish the job before he can move on. The killer has to prove—to himself and me—that he's smarter."

Her words hit him like a gut punch. "He won't stop coming for you."

She met his gaze. "No, Bennett, he won't."

Two hours later, Emilia sang the closing hymn of church service. Gorgeous wreaths wrapped in white lights hung around the cross and a Christmas tree sparkled in the corner, but there were no poinsettias. She was grateful. The bloom triggered her anxiety, and it would've been difficult to focus on the service.

She closed the hymn book and placed it in the cubby on the back of the pew. Bennett did the same. "Did you like the service?"

"I did. I know we have work to do, but it was nice to steal an hour away for church. It restores my heart and soul."

He nodded. "I agree. Even while working difficult cases, I try to slip away for service. It centers me."

Emilia remembered. Their common faith had bonded them while working on the task force together.

They'd attended church together on Sundays, and Emilia had missed having his company when she returned home.

In fact, she'd missed Bennett more than she wanted to admit. They'd only spent two days together, but it was like slipping back into a favorite shoe. Familiar and comforting. Easy. Even attending church together had felt as natural as breathing.

They'd taken their own vehicle to service, so Emilia waved goodbye to Bennett's family before stepping outside. The sun was shining brightly, but it did little to ease the bite of winter. Emilia adjusted her scarf before tucking the ends into her coat.

Bennett's gaze swept the parking lot. He tugged her closer to his side, and Emilia stiffened slightly. She surveyed the building surrounding them. There was no sign of danger, yet the threat lingered. Emilia had brief moments of normality, like inside church, but that was all. Stolen moments.

Bennett escorted her down the church steps, past the congregants gathered in small groups chitchatting. More than one head turned their way, including several pretty women.

Emilia leaned closer to Bennett and whispered, "It probably wasn't such a great idea for me to sit with you and your family during service."

"Why?"

"Didn't you hear all the breaking hearts when we walked in? You're going to have to do damage control next week with your admirers."

A flush crept across his cheeks. "I'm not interested in doing damage control. In fact, you may have saved me weeks of matchmaking. Everyone on this side of the Mason-Dixon line is trying to fix me up."

Emilia knew Bennett was divorced. He didn't talk about it much and she'd always sensed it was a painful topic. "You don't want to get married again?"

"I don't think about it. My life is busy with work, and my first marriage didn't end well. I'm not good at being a husband."

"I find that incredibly hard to believe. You're kind, hardworking, considerate. And you have an amazing family. I don't blame any of those women for trying to land you. You're a catch, Bennett."

He snorted. "If I'm such a catch, why didn't you try to land me?"

Emilia's heart clenched. A tangle of emotions warred within her, stealing her breath and her words.

Bennett seemed to realize exactly what he'd said because his flush deepened. "Never mind. Sorry, Emilia. We just got our friendship back on track and I'm mucking it up. Forget I said that."

He hurried a few steps ahead of her to open the passenger-side door of his truck. Embarrassment radiated off his movements. It would be smarter to leave the conversation there, but Emilia couldn't. It wasn't fair.

She circled the open door and stopped in front of him. "You are a catch, Bennett. And I've thought about trying to land you."

His gaze shot up and met hers. Emilia's breath

stalled. This close every one of the gold flecks buried in Bennett's eyes was visible. One step more and she'd be in his arms. It took everything in her to resist.

She fiddled with her scarf. "The problem is me. My parents weren't a good example of a functioning marriage. My dad was in and out of jail; my mom was an addict. They fought all the time. There was abuse and anger. Foster care left me bouncing from house to house. Love was a luxury I didn't have. Somewhere along the way, I guess, I lost my faith in it. At least...for myself."

Bennett was quiet for a long moment. He took Emilia's hand in his, running his thumb over her knuckles. Warmth spread up her arm.

"My wife left me the day before our wedding anniversary," Bennett said. "I had no idea she was unhappy in our marriage. Or maybe, Julie didn't want me to know. It took me a long time to realize we had different views on marriage. Our divorce was painful. I didn't think I'd be capable of risking my heart again. I'd also lost my faith in love."

"What changed your mind?"

"I met you." His lips curved into a smile. "You swept into town and blew me away with your brains and strength. Not to mention your beauty. For the first time since my divorce, I started thinking about a different future."

She sucked in a breath. No one had ever said such beautiful things to her. "Bennett, even if I could get past my family history..."

Derrick's attack had changed things. She was

plagued by memories and haunted by nightmares. The last year had been a constant struggle to put one foot in front of the other. Therapy had helped, but she still didn't feel normal. Emilia feared she never would.

Bennett released her hand. "Don't worry, Emilia. I know it's impossible. Serial killers and near-death experiences aren't part of your average love story."

No, they weren't. Emilia didn't know how to reconcile her feelings for Bennett with the horrors she'd endured. The threat against her wasn't even over. It was better to stick to their friendship and leave the rest behind.

"Are you sorry I said something?" Emilia asked.

"Not a bit, Em." He winked. "It's not every day a gorgeous woman tells me I'm irresistible."

She burst out laughing. "Oh, heavens. How are we going to fit your ego into the truck?"

Bennett's phone rang, cutting off any reply. He pulled it from his pocket. "Knox."

The sheriff's voice filtered out. Emilia couldn't distinguish the words, but Claire's tone was clipped and short.

Emilia's insides froze. She gripped the side of the truck door, the cold metal cutting into her palm. Bennett hung up and turned to face her. He didn't have to say anything. She already knew.

The killer struck again.

SIX

Bennett gripped the steering wheel with both hands as his truck flew down the freeway to the crime scene. In the passenger seat next to him, Emilia sat stiff and quiet.

The warmth of their earlier conversation was gone. Bennett didn't regret telling Emilia the truth about his feelings, but he needed to accept the reality of their situation. The relationship had nowhere to go. Bennett's life was in Fulton County. His job, his family, the ranch that had been worked by his grandparents and great-grandparents. It wasn't feasible for him to leave, and Bennett wouldn't blame Emilia for putting Fulton County in the rearview once this case was concluded.

Serial killers. It's what brought them together. It also tore them apart.

Bennett exited the freeway and steered his truck toward Creekside Park. His muscles tensed as the flashing lights of emergency vehicles came into view. He maneuvered as close to the entrance as possible before killing the engine.

Emilia reached for the door handle. Bennett placed a hand on her arm. "You don't have to do this. No one will think less of you if you don't."

"Thank you for saying that. But I do have to do this." Her mouth hardened and her eyes flashed with determination. "A woman is dead, and I will help find the man who did this and make sure he's put in jail for the rest of his life."

Bennett knew Emilia meant every word. It didn't matter the cost to herself. She would seek justice.

He admired her. For her strength and resilience.

They got out of the truck. The cold bit into Bennett's cheeks. He zipped up his coat, thankful for the thermal layering. As unlikely as it seemed for this part of Texas, there were predictions of snow for Christmas. Bennett held up the crime-scene tape and Emilia passed under it. They gave their names and rank to the deputy standing guard before heading toward the trail he indicated.

They trudged down the pathway until Claire came into view. The sheriff met them halfway. Her expression was grim.

"Thanks for coming so quickly." Claire's breath formed a cloud of condensation with each word. "Emilia, I'm sorry to ask this, but I need your expertise. Yours, too, Bennett. I need to know if we're dealing with a copycat or the original killer."

Bennett nodded. "Of course."

"Additionally, this murder appears to be connected to

the threat against Emilia. I'd like for us to continue working together."

He was grateful. Claire had primary jurisdiction and could make things difficult by being territorial. Instead, her focus was on getting justice and stopping a murderer. It was a complete turnaround from the former sheriff.

Bennett nodded again. "Anything you need, just ask. I'll assist in any way I can."

"Ditto," Emilia said. "And thank you, Sheriff, for keeping us in the loop."

"No need to thank me. We all have the same goal here: to catch the killer and put him in prison so he can never hurt anyone again." Claire led them to the body. "Our victim is Kathy Rose. Twenty-four. Works as a waitress for a diner near the freeway."

Bennett's chest tightened. Kathy was on her back, her hands positioned on her stomach. She was dressed in her underclothes. Cuts snaked down her arms and legs, and she'd been stabbed in the heart. In her hands was a poinsettia bloom.

Rage slipped through Bennett. Someone had taken this young woman's life in a brutal and terrifying way. All murder made him angry, but this...this was something else. His hands twitched. He ached to form fists and punch the nearest tree. But none of that would help.

Instead, he would channel his anger into finding Kathy's killer. She deserved justice.

He scanned the crime scene again. "The resemblance to the other victims is eerie. Same positioning of the body down to the poinsettia bloom, same cuts on her arms and legs."

Cuts that—Bennett knew—mirrored the scars Emilia had. A memory flashed in his mind of finding her hiding in the bushes near the lake, pale and icy cold. Near death. Bennett clamped down on the rush of emotions threatening to rise up. Emilia was alive. She'd survived. He needed to keep his focus on the woman who hadn't.

Emilia bent closer to the victim. Her expression was detached, a self-protection mechanism Bennett recognized. She was in cop mode.

"Same type of victim, dark-haired and pretty." Emilia sniffed the woman's skin without touching the body. "This isn't a copycat. Derrick had a partner. This is the work of the same killer from last year."

"How can you be sure?" Claire asked.

"There were certain things never shared outside the task force. For starters, the killer bleaches the bodies to remove trace evidence." She pointed to Kathy's feet. "Her toenails and fingernails have also been painted red. The killer did it before leaving her body here. Like the poinsettia, it's part of his ritual. How long has she been missing?"

"Kathy was last seen by her coworkers two nights ago." Claire glanced at the notebook in her hand. "Her car was found in the diner parking lot, but Kathy often leaves it there. Her apartment is within walking distance."

Bennett rocked back on his heels. "Why wasn't she reported missing?"

"No one realized she was. Kathy lives alone and had the last two days off from work. According to her boss, she's a homebody. It wasn't unusual for her car to stay in the parking lot for a couple of days while she caught up on her sleep and binged television."

"Who found her?"

"A local school teacher out for a hike with her dog." Claire waved her pen along the trail. "As you can tell, this area isn't used often. People normally stick to the paved pathways."

"The body hasn't been out here long," Bennett said. "Kathy was likely killed last night and placed on the trail in the early-morning hours."

Emilia nodded. "The killer kept her for a day or two. Also just like our original victims." She pointed to Kathy's shoulder. "Those marks appear to be from a stun gun. That's a new aspect to the crime. Derrick used drugs to subdue his victims when he kidnapped them."

Bennett frowned as he ran through what he knew about the other cases in his mind. "That makes sense if our theory about the case is right."

"Theory?" Claire asked.

"Derrick kidnapped the victims, but it was his partner who killed them." Bennett bent closer to examine the marks on Kathy's skin. Definitely a stun gun. "Derrick had a history of drug abuse. He had a supplier who provided the drugs which were used on the women."

"But now the killer is working alone," Emilia continued, picking up on Bennett's train of thought. "He doesn't have a connection to the drug dealer, so he needed a new way to subdue the victim. Hence the stun gun."

Claire scribbled a few notes in her pad. "How does last night's shooting fit into all of this? And the threatening note left on Emilia's doorstep?"

"The note was to bring me back to Fulton County." Emilia rose. "The shooting was an attempt to run Bennett off the road so the killer could grab me."

"But he already had Kathy. Why kidnap you too?"

"Opportunity. This killer is smart. He knows I'm going to be protected, and he was hoping to catch us off guard." She took a deep breath. The stark look in her expression was haunting. "If the killer is attempting a repeat of last year, then I'm supposed to be victim number four."

Her words slammed into Bennett with the force of a freight train. "He'll kill three more before you."

She nodded. "But that won't stop him from trying to grab me in the meantime. He's working off a game plan. The good thing is he doesn't have Derrick anymore. The killer has to stalk and kidnap the victims himself, which gives us a better opportunity to catch him."

Emilia turned to Claire. "Pull surveillance video from the diner where Kathy worked. Go back at least two weeks. The killer interacted with her. You're looking for a white male, 30-40, smart, well-dressed. He has a flexible schedule, which gives him the ability to stalk his victims. He's a killer but doesn't look like one. Nothing about him sets off alarm bells."

The sheriff jotted everything down in her notepad. "How long before he kidnaps the next victim?"

She shrugged. "There's no way to know for sure, but this killer is looking to make a splash. My best guess is we have days."

Bennett's stomach clenched. There was no time to waste.

"The killer's already identified his next victim. Stalked her." Emilia bit her lip. "Use the media to warn women to be careful. Ask them to call in anything suspicious, especially if they feel they're being followed."

"We'll get hundreds of tips."

"Yes, but we know this killer only likes pretty, single, dark-haired women. It's not much to go on, but it will help narrow the pool."

Claire nodded. "What else?"

"He has a place where he takes the victims." She glanced at the body. "It can't be far. Within a few hours' drive. Probably closer. The killer is from Fulton County or is extremely familiar with the area. Oh, and of course, he'll have a connection to Derrick."

Something rustled in the trees. Bennett peered into the woods. A man was lurking in the shadows of some bushes near the taped-off boundary securing the crime scene. The killer? It wasn't unusual for a murderer to revisit the scene of the crime.

"Police!" Bennett's hand went to his weapon. "Freeze!"

The man turned and ran.

Bennett bolted after him.

Emilia dashed after Bennett through the woods. Her boots slid over the pine needles and dry leaves. She pulled her weapon from the holster hidden along the small of her back. Ahead of them, a man dodged and weaved.

"Police!" Bennett shouted. "Freeze!"

The man paid them no heed. He picked up his pace, disappearing around a bend. Bennett muttered something before increasing his speed. The ground had a slight incline. Emilia's heart pounded and the cold air stung her lungs. Her heavy wool jacket and scarf slowed her progress.

Bennett rounded the bend, disappearing from view behind some foliage. A shout followed.

Bennett!

Emilia forced more power into her legs. She rounded the bush, gun raised. Two men rolled on the ground. Bennett and the man he'd been chasing. Emilia stepped closer, shouting. "Stop! Police!"

The warning seemed to register with the man in blue. He froze. Bennett whipped the man's hands behind his back and cuffed them. "You're under arrest."

"Wait!" the man shouted. "What are you doing? Hold on."

Something about the voice was familiar. Bennett hauled the man to his feet, and for the first time, Emilia got a look at his face. She inhaled sharply.

John McInnis. Derrick's former employer.

Claire came racing around the bend, gun in hand. She assessed the situation in three seconds and lowered her weapon.

Emilia lowered hers as well, but didn't holster it. John was cuffed, but that wasn't enough to prevent him from trying something. "You okay, Bennett?"

She scanned the Texas Ranger for injuries. He had a scrape on his cheek and mud stained his pants, but otherwise he looked fine. Anger hardened his handsome features.

"I'm okay." Bennett pushed John into a sitting position on a nearby fallen log. "What are you doing here, John?"

"In the park? I'm exercising." John's gaze flickered to Emilia and then to Bennett. His chest heaved and sweat coated the front of his shirt. "Can someone explain what on earth is going on? One minute, I'm exercising and the next I'm being tackled."

Emilia ignored his question. "What were you doing sneaking up to a crime scene?"

John's mouth dropped open. He blinked several times, giving the impression of a startled goldfish. "I didn't. I'm running in the park."

"You were near the crime-scene tape."

He shook his head as if struggling to comprehend her words. "What are you talking about? What crime-scene tape?" John struggled against the cuffs. "Get these off me. I haven't done anything wrong."

"You disobeyed an order to stop," Bennett said.

"I didn't *hear* an order to stop. I had my headphones

in." John jerked his chin at the ground. An earbud lay in the dirt.

Emilia retrieved it and held it up to her own ear. Loud rock music filtered out. A niggle of uncertainty tugged at her. Claire looked around and came up with a matching earbud a short distance away. They must've fallen out of John's ears in the tussle with Bennett.

"One of you, please explain to me what is going on?" John swallowed hard. "Wait...you said crime scene." His complexion paled, stark against the dark beard covering the lower half of his face. "Is this connected to Alice? And Derrick?"

"Yes." Emilia's hand closed around the earbud.

"I knew it was weird you were asking about Alice after so many years." John licked his lips. "Listen, guys, I run this route all the time. I zone out when I'm exercising. I didn't see the crime-scene tape and I didn't hear you order me to stop. The first time I heard police was when Emilia said it. I immediately did as I was ordered."

Bennett frowned. "This is your normal route through the park?"

"Yep. On weekdays, I run in the morning. But on Sunday, it's always in the afternoon. You can ask my secretary."

Was John lying? Or had the killer placed the body here on purpose knowing John would run past?

Claire stepped forward and took hold of John's arm. "All right. Come with me down to the sheriff's department. I want to get a full statement from you, along with a rundown of your activities for the last two days."

"Okay. No problem." He frowned. "But do you mind taking off the cuffs? I haven't done anything wrong. I honestly didn't know Bennett was a police officer when he tackled me. That's why I fought back."

Claire glanced at Bennett who nodded. "Go ahead."

Emilia agreed. There was no reason to keep John in cuffs. Technically, he hadn't committed a crime. It was better to have John continue cooperating with them.

Claire removed the cuffs and handed them back to Bennett before escorting John down the path. Emilia and Bennett followed at a distance. He dusted some pine needles off his shirt. "Well, these clothes are a total loss. Glad I have a spare set in my truck."

Emilia plucked a leaf from the collar of his shirt. "Nice takedown, by the way."

"Thanks." His lips curved into a smile. "Appreciate the backup. We make a good team, Emilia."

Warmth spread through her. They did make a good team.

Troopers and deputies milled about in the parking lot. Beyond the perimeter, reporters and onlookers chatted in groups. A little boy dodged the deputy standing guard and raced up to Emilia.

"Excuse me, ma'am." He thrust a small poinsettia plant toward her. "This is for you."

Emilia's heart stopped. A florist stick held a card with her name typed on it. From the killer? It had to be.

She lifted her gaze to the little boy's face. He was around eight, with big eyes hidden behind plastic-framed glasses. A chill raced down her spine at the thought of this innocent boy interacting with a cold-blooded murderer. "What's your name?"

"Peter, ma'am."

Emilia reached into her pocket and removed her leather gloves. She slipped one on and took the plant from him. "Where did you get this, Peter?"

"Some guy sitting over there in a ball cap." He pointed to a picnic table several yards away. The bench was empty, and no one was standing nearby.

"Can you tell me what the man looked like?"

"No. He was wearing a ball cap and had a scarf around his face. But he told me I had to give this plant to the lady in a purple scarf and black jacket." Peter's brows dipped down. "That's you, right? Because he paid me twenty dollars and I have to make sure I get it right."

"It's me."

She scanned the crowd. The killer had been here. Watching. Might still be, although he was smart enough to have changed his appearance so Peter wouldn't recognize him. Her throat tightened.

Bennett briefly touched Emilia, his palm flat against her back. A silent but gentle reminder that she wasn't alone. She was grateful for it.

Emilia focused back on Peter. "How long ago was this? When did you talk to the man?"

Peter shrugged. "Don't know. I was riding my bike, and he asked me to deliver the plant."

Bennett waved a deputy over and had a hushed conversation. Emilia asked Peter some more questions, but the little boy couldn't provide any further explanation. The killer had done a good job masking both his facial features and his voice.

When Bennett appeared back at her side accompanied by the deputy, Emilia said, "Okay, Peter. This policeman is going to take you back to your parents now."

The little boy shifted in his dirty tennis shoes. "Am I in trouble?"

"No. Not at all." Emilia forced herself to smile. "And the deputy will make sure your parents understand that."

The deputy nodded. He patted Peter on the back. "Come on. Let's find your folks."

They walked across the parking lot.

Emilia was still holding the poinsettia, but at arm's length as though it was a bomb. Her stomach ached.

Bennett pulled a set of gloves out of his pocket. He slipped them on. "Here, give it to me."

She gladly handed the plant over. Emilia took a deep breath and removed the envelope. The flap wasn't sealed. Carefully, she slid the card out, her fingers trembling slightly. The message was also typewritten. Reading it iced her blood.

I'm watching.
I'm coming for you, my pet.
I promise.

SEVEN

Two hours later, Emilia sipped coffee, but the warm liquid didn't dispel the chill in her bones. The killer was still out there and he was coming for her. Worse, if they didn't stop him, he'd murder three other women.

She couldn't let that happen. She wouldn't.

Emilia gripped the coffee mug. The Fulton County Sheriff's Department was a buzz of activity. The sheriff had called in extra hands to process the crime scene and track down leads. Emilia weaved her way through the bullpen to the observation room. The door was cocked open, and she slipped inside.

Bennett stood in front of the one-way glass watching John pace the interview room. The business man had given an initial statement and agreed to wait while the information was verified. John was still dressed in his running clothes. Mud stained his shirt and pants from the tangle with Bennett.

Emilia leaned against the wall. Bennett had changed

into fresh pants and a new button-down shirt from a spare set he carried in his truck. The scent of his after-shave wafted toward her. Emilia breathed it in and the tension in her shoulders loosened.

She took another sip of coffee. "The news was on in the break room. Someone leaked details about the murder to the media. They've connected Kathy's death to the ones from last year. The reporter theorized that Derrick was not the Holiday Slasher."

Bennett scowled. "I hate that name. The Holiday Slasher. It gives the killer notoriety, which is exactly what he wants."

He was right. She hated the nickname too.

Bennett raked a hand through his hair. "This is going to be a media circus."

"No use crying over spilled milk. We'll just have to deal with it. Did you arrange for a sketch artist to sit down with Peter?"

"Yes. We should have something by tonight. The poinsettia along with the note have been sent to the state lab as well, although I don't think they'll get prints from either item. The killer is smart enough to have worn gloves."

Claire walked into the room. She closed the door behind her. "I spoke to John's secretary, Velma. She verified John runs on that path every day, including Sunday. Weekdays, it's in the morning. Sunday, it's in the afternoon. He's strict with his schedule and exercises like clockwork. I also asked about Derrick Jackson. According to Velma, John and Derrick regularly had lunch together. She described them as friendly."

Bennett rocked back on his heels. "John didn't tell us that in our first interview with him. He claimed to barely know Derrick."

Emilia jerked her chin toward the one-way glass. "John could've given the letter to Peter before hitting the running trail."

"He consented to a search of his car," Claire said. "We didn't find a hat or scarf. I've also got deputies searching the trash and area around the parking lot, but so far we've come up empty-handed. There's no indication John is the same man who approached Peter. Besides, if he's the killer, why run right past the crime scene? It draws our attention to him, which seems counterproductive."

"Arrogance." Emilia kept her gaze on John still pacing the interview room. "The killer is confident, Sheriff. He's not afraid to take risks. What else do we know about John?"

"His criminal record is clean. Business finances are in good shape. Both parents are deceased, and he doesn't have any siblings. John's secretary described him as demanding but a fair boss." Claire crossed her arms. "He doesn't have an alibi for Kathy's disappearance or her murder. John lives alone, so no one can verify he was there."

"I want to interview him." Emilia turned to Bennett. "Alone, this time. It'll be easier to study his reaction to being around me."

His mouth flattened, but he nodded. "We'll be here watching."

She met his gaze for a moment. Warmth spread through her chest. Bennett wanted to protect her, but he didn't try to talk her out of interviewing John. He knew when to treat her like a friend and when to treat her as a professional. She appreciated the delicate balance.

Emilia squared her shoulders and took a deep breath before entering the interview room.

John paused in his pacing midstep. "Oh, thank goodness. Have you spoken to my secretary? Did she confirm I normally run on that trail?"

"Yes, Mr. McInnis, she did." Emilia gestured to a chair. "Please, take a seat. I have a few more questions. But first, I'm going to review your rights."

She ran through the Miranda warning. John had signed away his rights earlier when he was questioned by Claire, but Emilia wanted to make sure any information gathered in this interview was admissible in court.

John continued to stand. "More questions? Why? I've already told Sheriff Hanks everything. Honestly, I had no idea I was near a crime scene."

"Things are more complicated. Please, take a seat, sir."

John did as she requested. He jabbed his hands through his hair, making it stand on end. "Is this about Derrick?"

"It is. We believe Derrick wasn't acting alone when he committed the murders last year."

Since the media had already connected the deaths,

Emilia wasn't telling Derrick anything he wouldn't discover when he left the interview room. At least, now she could use it to her advantage.

John blinked at her. "What do you mean Derrick wasn't working alone?"

"He had a partner. Someone he killed with."

Some emotion flashed in John's eyes, but before Emilia could distinguish what, it disappeared. Still, the hair on the back of her neck rose.

John's gaze dropped to the table. He shook his head. "That's horrible."

"It is. Do you know Kathy Rose?"

"She's a waitress over at the Milly's Diner off the freeway. I go there sometimes after work. Sweet lady..." He sucked in a sharp breath. "Oh no. Kathy's dead?"

"She was murdered by Derrick's partner. That's the crime scene you ran close to this morning, Mr. McInnis. It seems an unlikely coincidence that her body was left on the trail you frequent."

His mouth dropped open. "You can't think I'm involved? That's preposterous."

"Is it?" She arched her brows. "You and Derrick regularly had lunch together. In our first meeting, you claimed to barely know him. You lied to me."

"Wait, wait, wait." He held up his hands. "I didn't lie. Derrick and I weren't close. Yes, we had lunch together sometimes, but I do the same with all of my employees. It's an opportunity to speak to them in a nonformal setting."

The man had an answer for everything.

Emilia pushed harder. "Here's the problem, Mr. McInnis. I can connect you to three of the victims. You dated Alice Nelson. Rachel McAdams lived in an apartment complex your company manages. And now, Kathy Rose. You also had a relationship with Derrick."

John continued to study the table, but his eyes flickered back and forth as if he was sorting through a puzzle. His breathing increased. "I...I don't think it was a coincidence Kathy was left on the same running trail I use." He met her gaze. "But I swear, I didn't have anything to do with her death. I'm being set up."

"Set up? Why would the killer do that?"

"Because of what I know." His hands trembled. John licked his lips. "Here's the thing. Derrick didn't have any family or many friends. He was a loner."

She stayed quiet, letting John find his way to the point. Emilia didn't want him to stop talking. She'd felt from their first meeting John was withholding important information about the case.

"When I started taking him out to lunch, Derrick would talk to me about stuff. Sometimes we talked about his family." John swallowed hard. "Derrick has a brother. Here in Fulton County."

Emilia froze. Her pulse thundered in her ears. "Derrick told you that?"

He nodded. "It's a secret because the brother was put up for adoption before Derrick was born. Derrick found out about him from his grandmother before she died. Almost no one else knows."

"Who is Derrick's brother?"

"Malcolm King. Sheriff King's son."

Malcolm King lived on several acres on the outskirts of town. The property was close enough to provide privacy while still being only a fifteen-minute drive to his law practice. The sun was setting as Bennett crossed the yard toward the barn. Brilliant pinks and purples painted the sky with bold colors. On a normal day, Bennett might take a moment to admire the gorgeous sight. But not today.

Exhaustion bore down on his shoulders, but a determination to get to the truth fueled his steps. Was Malcolm really Derrick's brother? Malcolm's adoption wasn't a secret, but the King family had always said his birth parents were dead. Derrick was one year younger and had been raised by his maternal grandparents. It was entirely possible Malcolm and Derrick were related but had only discovered the truth as adults.

If they were brothers, did Sheriff King know? The former sheriff had been in a hurry to dissolve the task force after Derrick's death. The case files had holes. Mistakes had been made. Bennett had always believed those errors were due to sloppy police work. Now he was considering they'd been done on purpose.

Malcolm came into view. He was standing on a ladder. His workman's overalls were spattered with red paint and a ball cap covered his dirty blond hair. Extra rollers along with a bucket of paint rested on a tarp nearby. He lifted a hand in greeting. "Hey, Bennett."

"Hi, Malcolm. Sorry to drop in like this, but I need to speak to you."

Emilia had wanted to come along, but Bennett convinced her to stay back. He was friendly with Malcolm. The two had been bull riders together, and there was a rapport between them. The questions that needed to be asked were sensitive. Bennett hoped Malcolm would feel more comfortable being honest if they were alone.

Malcolm descended the ladder, and it rattled with his heavy weight. "What can I do for you?"

Bennett had twisted and turned different ways to approach this in his mind. He decided to ease into things. "Ignite Development. The corporation is a client of yours, correct?"

"Yes." Malcolm reached for a cloth and wiped paint off his hands.

"Ignite bought the property previously owned by Derrick Jackson. I'd like to request access to conduct a search on the land."

Malcolm didn't miss a beat. "Does this have anything to do with the murdered woman y'all found in the park today? I heard on the news that it looks like the ones from last year. Speculation is that Derrick wasn't the Holiday Slasher after all."

"Derrick was working with a partner."

Sheriff Hanks would give a news conference in an hour regarding the case. Bennett saw no reason to hold back in his conversation with Malcolm, since it would be public knowledge in short order.

Malcolm's eyes widened. "Interesting. Pop will be upset to hear that."

Bennett had no intention of bringing Sheriff King into this conversation. He steered it back to the matter at hand. "There may be evidence on Derrick's old property that could aid our search for his partner."

"I don't see how. Derrick's cabin was torn down shortly after Ignite bought the property. The owner wants to develop the land into an upscale residential neighborhood."

"Access would be helpful, even if the cabin is gone."

Malcolm's gaze narrowed. "You're looking for more victims?" He waved a hand. "Never mind. You can't tell me that. My dad was sheriff long enough for me to know better than to ask questions about an active investigation."

"Who is the owner of Ignite Development?"

Malcolm bent to retrieve a roller from the tarp. "You know full well I can't tell you that. It's covered under attorney/client privilege. I will forward your request to my client, but don't hold your breath, Bennett. I don't think he'll agree."

"Why not?"

"He doesn't allow anyone on the land for any reason. Not even me. The only reason I know the cabin is torn down is because the client told me it was."

Bennett rocked back in his heels. "And you don't find

that suspicious? That he won't let anyone on the property?"

"It's weird, sure. But I've had stranger issues with clients. I recommend you get a warrant."

Bennett didn't have enough probable cause for a warrant. A judge had already turned him down. Now Malcolm had too. Did his friend really have a client? Or was Malcolm the true owner of Ignite? Bennett had no way to find out.

It was time to switch gears. Bennett kept his gaze locked on Malcolm's face. "There's something else I need to discuss with you."

"Go for it." Malcolm steered the paint roller through the liquid in the tray.

"Are you Derrick Jackson's brother?"

Malcolm froze. A flush rose from his collar to stain his cheeks, but he didn't look at Bennett. "Who told you that?"

"It doesn't matter. Is it true?"

Malcolm rose. His expression was hard. "I thought you were my friend. I see now you're nothing more than a rumor monger. My parents are Larry and Carol King. I don't have any siblings. None. You got that?"

"Malcolm—"

"Shut it, Bennett. I'm not an idiot. My father was the sheriff of this town for thirty years. I know exactly what you're doing. Don't think for one second you are going to pin these murders on me."

He flung the roller at the barn. It hit the wall of the building with a thump and red paint spattered everywhere. Bennett had never seen his friend so angry or rattled. Malcolm was known for being calm and controlled, even under stressful circumstances. It's what made him an excellent bull rider and, later, attorney.

Maybe Bennett didn't know Malcolm as well as he thought.

Malcolm's hands formed into fists. "We're done here. Get off my land, Bennett. If you have any other questions, call my personal attorney."

EIGHT

The conversation with Malcolm plagued Bennett all the way home, while eating dinner with his family, and even during decorating the Christmas tree. A headache crept across his temples and his back muscles were tight with tension. The more he thought about the case, the more questions he had.

"Stop scowling." Emilia elbowed him. "You look like the Grinch."

Bennett blinked, jerked from his thoughts, and took in the scene unfolding in the living room. His father detangled lights while his mother unwrapped ornaments. Sage and her family were adding tinsel to the Christmas tree. Liz, pigtails bobbing, wriggled with excitement. Her grin couldn't get any wider.

Bennett shook his head and turned back to Emilia. "Sorry. My mind is working overtime."

"I know. Mine too. But I don't want to ruin this for your family. They're having a great time."

She'd been through an ordeal over the last few days, and yet Emilia still thought of Bennett's family. The woman was downright amazing. Brave, smart, caring. Not to mention drop-dead gorgeous. Emilia's dark hair flowed loose over her shoulders, and she was wearing a red sweater, which highlighted the natural color in her cheeks. Bennett was tempted to touch the creamy skin along her collarbone.

Lord, I'm going to fall in love with her at this rate. Help me get through this with my heart intact.

Bennett tore his gaze from Emilia and eyed the popcorn strand they were making for the tree. It wasn't even half done. He reached into the bowl and retrieved a kernel of popcorn before carefully threading it.

Emilia attempted to do the same on her side, but the popcorn broke in half. She smiled ruefully. "I'm not very good at this."

"There's a trick to it." Bennett grabbed another kernel and handed it to her. "Thread it through the center."

She made a second attempt and again the popcorn broke. Emilia blew out a frustrated breath.

Bennett's mouth curved up. "You're trying too hard. This isn't war, Emilia. You don't have to force the popcorn onto the strand."

He took another kernel and then her hand. Her palm was warm, the bones delicate and feminine. Bennett's heart skipped a beat. Together, they threaded a kernel onto the strand. It stayed in one piece, slipping on the dental floss easily.

"Better watch out, Bennett. Now I know your secret."

Emilia's eyes sparkled with mischievousness. "Apparently, everyone in the family is upset that you always string the most popcorn garland. Your mom promised me extra apple cider if I beat you this time."

Bennett burst out laughing. "It'll never happen, Em."

"Uncle B, Uncle B." Liz appeared at his side. "Can you help me put the star on the tree? You're the tallest person in the family."

Bennett smiled at his niece. "Sure thing, kiddo."

For the next hour, they continued with the tree. Lights, popcorn garland, and ornaments. Holiday music filtered from the speakers and a fire blazed in the hearth. It was homey, and by the time the tree was finished, Bennett's headache had faded.

The living room emptied little by little. Sage and her crew went home. Zeke was suffering from a head cold and, after saying goodnight, went to bed. Bennett helped his mom carry the last of the dessert dishes into the kitchen.

"There's more apple cider for you and Emilia to share." Joanna set plates into the sink. "Oh, and a box came for you today. I set it on the bookshelf next to the door."

"Thanks." He smiled at his mom. "Go to bed. I'll handle the dishes. You look tired."

She patted his cheek. "You're a good son. Love you."

"Love you too."

He made quick work of the dishes before pouring the apple cider into two mugs and carrying them back into the living room.

Emilia was standing next to the window, watching the lights on the tree flicker. She smiled at him. "We did a good job, didn't we?"

"Yes. It looks great." He handed her a mug. "Here, apple cider."

She took the cup and thanked him. Bennett set his down on the coffee table before retrieving the delivery box from the bookshelf. He opened it, removing a bracelet. It had a simple round charm with a cross etched on it. "I have something for you."

Emilia's brows arched at the sight of the jewelry in his hand. "You bought me a bracelet?"

"It's a safety device. The charm has a GPS tracker inside."

He undid the clasp and wrapped it around her wrist. The sleeve of her sweater rode up revealing the faded scar on her silky skin. Bennett brushed the old wound with his thumb. "The bracelet is a last resort. We shouldn't have to use it—"

Emilia stepped forward and dropped her forehead to his chest. Her face was hidden behind a waterfall of hair. Bennett felt the shuddering intake of her breath. His heart broke into a thousand pieces when he realized she was crying.

He wrapped his arms around her. "It's going to be okay."

"I know." She backed out of his embrace, swiping at her cheeks. "I'm sorry. I don't know what came over me."

Bennett did. The last several days had been a whirl-wind of pain and heartache, constant reminders of everything she went through last year. Seeing the crime scene this morning and receiving a note from the killer had to be terrifying.

"Emilia, I'm here. For whatever you need, even if it's a shoulder to cry on."

She hesitated and then stepped closer. Bennett embraced her. "Come here, Em."

Emilia melted into him. Her tears dampened the fabric of his shirt as sobs shook her slender shoulders.

Bennett rubbed her back in soothing motions. It was tearing him to pieces to know she was in pain. He wanted to take it from her but couldn't. The only thing he could do was this. Be there. Hold her. Walk through it with her.

Her tears quieted, but Emilia didn't back out of his arms. She kept her head on his chest. "Thank you for the bracelet. For letting me stay here. For everything. It means more to me than you will ever know."

His heart twisted and nearly broke at the tremble in her voice. "You don't need to thank me, Em. And just for the record, you're always welcome here."

A slow Christmas tune came on the radio. Bennett took Emilia's hand in his and started dancing. She sighed with pleasure and hummed along. The fireplace kept the room warm and the Christmas lights from the tree blazed color across the carpet.

When the song was over, Emilia lifted her head. Their gazes caught and held. Bennett's heart stopped and then took off. He could drown in the warmth of her eyes. His head dipped closer on pure instinct, his attention drawn to her lips.

Emilia jerked out of his embrace, nearly tripping over the coffee table in her haste to get away from him. Her face grew flushed. "Our apple cider is getting cold."

Bennett blinked, the spell between them broken. His mind caught up with his heart in a flash. What on earth was he doing? He'd almost kissed Emilia.

"Right." He cleared his throat. "The apple cider."

Bennett retrieved his cup with jerky movements and took a sip. The sweet liquid was lukewarm. He struggled to settle his heart rate. Kissing Emilia would've been a gigantic mistake. It would've complicated a relationship already struggling to stay balanced. Hadn't they decided this morning—was it just this morning?—that a relationship was impossible. It seemed Bennett's heart hadn't gotten the memo.

Emilia nestled in the corner of the couch. "What are your thoughts about Malcolm?"

The case was solid ground for them to fall back on. Bennett was relieved she'd transitioned to it. Emilia didn't seem upset about their near kiss, and he was happy to move on without drawing more attention to it.

He sat on the recliner facing Emilia. "Malcolm's reaction to my questions is bugging me. I've never seen him get so upset. He was furious."

"Well, Derrick is a serial killer. Being linked to him isn't something most people would sign up for."

"True, but I keep thinking about the hurried way the case was closed last year. And when I spoke to Sheriff King about the threat against you, he was adamant it wasn't connected to Derrick. Were those judgment errors? Or is Randy hiding his son's involvement in the murders?"

She wrinkled her nose. "There's also Ignite Development. Who owns it? I don't think it's a coincidence that Malcolm is the attorney for the corporation." She was quiet for a moment. "Do you think John is muddying the waters of this case by pointing the finger at Malcolm?"

It was an interesting thought. "That's possible. I don't trust John. He's lied about his relationship with Derrick and he's connected to several of the victims."

"He also doesn't have an alibi for last night. Trouble is, we don't have any physical evidence linking him to the murders. Claire is interviewing Kathy's friends and family hoping it'll lead to a break in the case."

Bennett's phone beeped with a loud siren. He yanked it from his pocket. A message with a red alert and coordinates flashed across the screen.

"What is it?" Emilia asked.

"Someone is attempting to breach the ranch gate."

Emilia's heart leapt into her throat and then slid back down to her chest, beating out a rapid tempo. "Which gate? The front one?"

"No. The rear entrance. Hold on, we have cameras."

Bennett tapped on his phone, bringing up the video. Emilia leaned over his arm to see. She inhaled sharply. "Randy King. What on earth is he doing?"

The former sheriff was rattling the gate in a rage.

Then he kicked it. His truck appeared to be running behind him, the headlights illuminating the surrounding area.

Bennett's jaw tightened. "I don't know what he's doing, but I intend to find out."

She followed Bennett to the front door, snagging her coat from the rack. "You aren't going without backup. I'm coming with you."

"Absolutely not. There's no danger, Emilia. Sheriff King isn't going to hurt me."

"Unless it's a trap." She shoved on her boots. "We don't know the extent of Malcolm or his father's connection to Derrick. They could be hiding a relationship with him. Or we stumbled into something we don't understand yet. Sheriff King didn't show up on your property at midnight for tea and cookies. He's obviously angry."

Bennett grabbed his own jacket. "I interviewed Malcolm alone."

"Which I objected to, if you remember. Besides, that was a calculated risk. You were hoping he would tell you the truth. This is different."

She keyed in the code on the gun safe in the foyer closet and removed her service weapon. Emilia checked to ensure it was loaded.

"Don't be stubborn, Bennett. I saw the images of your truck from the shooting a few nights ago. The killer was aiming for you. He's looking to get revenge. Or he wants you dead so he can get to me. Either way, your life is at risk as much as mine. It's smart to do this together."

He paused and then nodded. "You're right."

Bennett removed his own gun from the safe and holstered it. They slipped into the wintery night and headed for Bennett's truck. The windshield was frosted over.

Emilia shivered inside her coat. She hadn't bothered to holster her gun. Instead she gripped it in her hand, taking comfort in the familiar weight. The truck rumbled to life and flew down the main driveway.

Within short order, they were on the dark country road that wrapped around the ranch. Emilia's gaze swept across the woods, searching for any potential threats. Maybe it was an overreaction. After all, Sheriff King had been a lawman until his forced retirement due to Parkinson's. But something inside whispered to stay on her guard. She wouldn't ignore her instincts.

"There he is," Bennett muttered, as the black truck came into view. "Stay back, Emilia, and cover me."

He stopped the vehicle. Emilia jumped from the seat and used the open passenger-side door as a shield. Adrenaline flooded her veins, but her hands were steady and her movements sure. She kept her weapon ready as Bennett rounded the front of the truck and called out, "Sheriff King."

Randy came into view of the headlights. His hair was disheveled and one pant leg was hooked on the top of his boot. He carried a shotgun. "'Bout time you showed up, boy."

Bennett stopped, his hand going to the holster on his hip, but didn't draw his weapon. There was no need for him to. Emilia had a clear shot and she would keep him safe. The weight of Bennett's trust settled on her shoulders like a warm cloak. He didn't just respect her as a woman, but as a cop too. It mattered.

Regret rippled through Emilia. Bennett had nearly kissed her tonight. She'd wanted him to, but panic set in at the last minute. The handsome Texas Ranger was wheedling his way past her defenses and into her heart.

Please, Lord. Watch over us, especially Bennett.

"You need to stay away from my son." Randy raised his shotgun slightly. "Do you understand me, Ranger? Don't come near my boy asking questions about Derrick Jackson. Malcolm doesn't know anything about that killer."

Randy's words were slightly slurred. Parkinson's affected the nervous system, so it could be a product of his disease. Or perhaps the former sheriff had been drinking. Either way, waving the shotgun around was asking for trouble. He could accidentally shoot Bennett.

Emilia kept her breathing steady and her weapon fixed on the older man. It took all of her training to keep her muscles from locking up with tension.

"Sir, I meant no disrespect when I spoke to Malcolm." Bennett's voice was calm. "Put down your shotgun and we can talk about it."

"There ain't nothing to talk about. You're trying to ruin my son. I won't have it. How dare you, Bennett? How dare you suggest my son and Derrick were brothers?"

Bennett slid closer. "Sir, you need to put down your shotgun."

"I don't need to do nothin'." Randy's face flushed, and he raised the weapon, bracing it against his shoulder. "You need to listen."

Emilia held her breath. She didn't want to shoot the former sheriff, especially if he was in an altered state, but she would if it was necessary to save Bennett's life. She sent up another prayer.

Bennett raised his hands in the classic sign of surrender. "I'm listening, Sheriff King. You have my complete attention."

"Derrick showed up at our house years ago, spewing garbage about being related to Malcolm. It was a lie. There's no way the two men can be related. I kicked him off our property and warned him about spreading false rumors. I thought Derrick had listened, but he must've told someone. Now you're giving those nasty lies new attention."

"It's not my intention to hurt your son, Sheriff King."

Randy swayed slightly, lowering the shotgun barrel to the ground. "You should've come to me to ask your questions. I know there's been another murder. I've got something that can help with the case."

"I would love to get your input, Sheriff. But first you have to put down your shotgun." Bennett offered a strained smile. "We can't have a conversation like this. What would your wife say?"

Randy glanced down at the weapon. He seemed almost surprised to find it in his hands. "Oh yes. Carol would be very upset. She'd say it was uncivilized. She never did like guns much."

He lowered it to the ground, nearly tripping over his own feet as he did so.

Bennett caught the older man before he hit the ground. "There we are, Sheriff."

Emilia breathed out a sigh of relief. She rounded the truck door and took control of the shotgun. Sheriff King's behavior tonight was completely out of character. Had Randy been drinking? Or taking drugs?

Randy leaned heavily on Bennett. "I don't feel so good."

Sheriff King was growing paler by the second. It was clear something was medically wrong with him. Emilia grabbed the older man's wrist and felt his pulse. It was strong, but Randy looked ready to pass out.

"Let's get him to the hospital," Bennett whispered to Emilia. "I'd call an ambulance but driving him will be faster. Can you lock up his truck while I load him in mine?"

Emilia nodded. She circled Randy's vehicle and opened the door. The scent of stale cigarettes slapped her in the face. She killed the engine and flipped off the headlights.

A photograph tucked in the dash caught her attention. It was crisp, as if it'd been recently removed from a photo album. A woman stood between two men. Emilia's heart skittered as recognition sank into her.

The woman was Alice Nelson. She was smiling widely and held a plastic cup containing some kind of drink. On her right side, his arm looped over her shoulders, was Derrick. A date was stamped on the bottom of the photograph. It'd been taken the evening Alice disappeared.

A second man stood back from Alice and Derrick, almost in the shadows. His blond hair was slicked back, and he had a lanky build. If Emilia hadn't run into him at the hospital recently, she might not have recognized him. But she did.

Henry Stillman.

NINE

Morning sunlight streamed through the trees and dew coated the grass. Bennett stifled a yawn and guzzled a cup of coffee. His eyes felt gritty from lack of sleep. He'd hoped the brisk outside air would refresh him, but that wasn't the case.

The screen door behind him creaked open and then slammed shut. His sister, Sage, appeared at his side on the porch, sipping her own cup of coffee. "Gorgeous morning."

"It is. Sneaking over to steal mom's coffee again?"

"She makes it better than I do. If you're waiting for Emilia, she's already awake and working in your office. I saw her when I put a few horses out to pasture."

"Does that woman ever sleep? We didn't get home from the hospital till after one."

"She's under a lot of stress. So are you." Sage leaned against the porch pillar. "I heard Malcolm may be involved. Is that why Sheriff King was knocking on our gate last night?"

"Yes. We've stumbled into a hornet's nest of rumors and innuendo, and I'm not sure how it fits in with the murders." He drained his cup and handed it to his sister. "Mind taking that inside for me?"

"Not at all. Hey, when all of this is over, what are the chances Emilia will visit for Christmas? The entire family adores her." Sage arched her brows. "And unless I'm wrong, so do you."

"You're not wrong, but things are complicated. Fulton County holds bad memories for her, and I'm a part of that."

Sage was quiet for a long moment. "Have you told her you're in love with her?"

His sister's question rocked him. Was he in love with Emilia? He hadn't given himself permission to even consider it. "She knows I care."

"Want a bit of advice?"

His mouth twitched. "Do I have a choice?"

Sage chuckled. "Not really, no." Her expression grew serious. "God put Emilia in your life for a reason, Bennett. Put your trust in that and have faith that everything will work out the way it's supposed to. Don't hold back because you're scared."

It was sound advice. Bennett had been holding back. His divorce had left him scarred and wary, but he was tired of fighting his feelings for Emilia. Maybe it was time to surrender, risk the broken heart, and let God take care of the rest.

Bennett hugged his sister. "Thanks, Sage."

"Anytime." She planted a kiss on his cheek. "Love you. Try not to get shot between now and the next time I see you."

He chuckled. "I'll do my best."

Bennett crossed the yard to the barn. The main doors on either side of the building were wide open, letting in sunshine and fresh air. A horse whinnied at the sound of Bennett's boots on the concrete. He greeted the animal with a pat before heading to his office.

Emilia was sitting at his desk, studying something on the computer. Her hair was pulled back into a low ponytail, but a few loose strands played with her cheeks. She wasn't wearing makeup. It only accented her natural beauty.

Bennett's dog, Duke, lay at Emilia's feet. The lazy mutt opened one eye, checked to make sure there was no danger, and then promptly went back to sleep.

"What are you reading?" Bennett stepped into the office.

"Henry Stillman's criminal record." Emilia lifted the photograph she'd found in Sheriff King's truck. "He's the other guy in this picture. Do you remember we ran into him at the hospital on the night of the shooting? He came into the room with my discharge paperwork."

Bennett remembered him well because Emilia had been distinctly uncomfortable in Henry's presence. "You were in a foster home with him, right?"

"For a brief time when I was thirteen." Her nose

wrinkled. "He was a troublemaker and had a mean streak."

"Can you give me an example?"

"He would steal things and then blame other foster kids, he liked to frighten the younger kids by jumping out at them." Her expression hardened. "I defended the little ones, and he turned his attention to me. He set fire to my homework. Snuck into the bathroom while I was taking a shower—the lock was broken at the time—and stole my clothes and the towel. Henry never physically hurt anyone, but he was cruel. And he took pleasure in making other people miserable."

Bennett couldn't imagine. His home had always been a place of love and kindness. Emilia's childhood had been the complete opposite, as this incident illustrated. It explained so much about their conversation the other day. Emilia had lost faith in love because she'd never had it in the first place. Perhaps, deep down, Emilia wasn't sure she deserved it. Bennett vowed to prove her wrong.

Turning his attention back to the task at hand, Bennett gestured to the computer. "Any arrests?"

Emilia turned the monitor so he could see the screen. "Several arrests in his twenties for assault, domestic battery, and DUIs. Most of the charges were dropped. He only went to jail once, for the second DUI."

Bennett scanned the reports. "After that, it looks like Henry cleaned up his act."

"Or he got smarter. Sometimes, criminals go into jail and learn from each other."

"True." Bennett pulled a chair around next to her

and studied the whiteboard on the wall. They had a lot of pieces, but none of the puzzle was making sense. "The photograph was taken on the night Alice disappeared. Sheriff King mentioned when I initially spoke to him that she'd gone to a party."

"But why did he have possession of this picture? Why wasn't it in Alice's case file? And how does Henry tie into this? For that matter, how does Malcolm?" She rubbed her temples. "We have too many suspects and not enough hard evidence."

Bennett's phone rang. He pulled it from his pocket, surprise rippling through him at the name flashing on his screen. Sheriff King.

Bennett answered, putting the call on speaker. "Knox."

"Morning, Bennett." Randy's voice was scratchy, so unlike his normal thunderous boom. "Hope I didn't catch you at a bad time."

"No, sir. How are you feeling?"

"Better. In fact, I'm being released from the hospital. I'd like to stop by your place and pick up my truck. Can you meet me at the gate? And bring Emilia. I'd like to speak to both of you."

"You can come up to the house—"

"No. I don't want to bother your folks any more than I already have."

Bennett caught the thread of embarrassment running through the other man's voice. He decided not to push the issue. "Okay. What time?"

"Twenty minutes all right?"

"Fine. See you then." Bennett hung up and picked up the photograph. "We might get some answers to our questions after all."

Emilia absently played with the GPS bracelet Bennett had given her. Her fingers trailed over the cross. "I'm surprised. I didn't think Sheriff King would talk to us. Malcolm invoked his right to counsel when Claire tried to question him last night."

"Sheriff King may be doing damage control. We'll have to see. Want to horseback ride out to the gate? It's a pretty day, and I don't know about you, but I could use some sunshine."

A smile broke across Emilia's face, wiping away the exhaustion. "That sounds fantastic. I haven't been riding in ages and a little exercise would clear my head."

She tugged on her shirtsleeve and stood.

Bennett caught her hand. "You don't have to cover your scars around me. I hope you know that."

A soft look came into her eyes. "I do know that." Emilia shrugged. "It's a habit. People stare and ask questions. It's difficult to explain. Kinda like my childhood. I've gotten used to hiding the ugly parts about myself."

"Your childhood and your scars aren't ugly. They're proof of your resilience and your strength."

Emilia lifted her head. Tears shimmered in her eyes. One dropped off her lashes onto her cheek.

Bennett's heart sank. "I'm sorry. I didn't mean to upset you."

"No, please don't apologize. It's just...you say the most beautiful things to me."

She cupped his face with her hand, her thumb running along the stubble on his cheek. Bennett's breath stalled. Emilia's touch sent warm heat arcing through him. He didn't dare move for fear of ruining the sweet moment.

Emilia stood on her tiptoes and brushed her mouth against his lips. The kiss was featherlight and left him aching for more. She pulled back slightly but didn't leave his embrace. Their gazes met and the desire in her eyes matched his own.

Bennett didn't hesitate. He claimed her mouth, giving in to the emotion and letting go of his fears. Emilia melted against him, her body soft against his, and Bennett's heart rate skyrocketed. The woman left him undone and muddled his thinking. She also never ceased to amaze him.

Bennett knew in that moment he was a goner. In love. Was there a future for them? He had no idea. In that second, he didn't care.

He would love her with everything he had until she told him to stop.

———

Fifteen minutes later, Emilia's side hurt from laughing. She dismounted the pretty black-and-white mare. "I did not cheat. I won the race across the pasture fair and square."

Bennett scowled playfully as he tied his horse's reins

to a branch. "You didn't wait until I finished. It's one, two, three, go. You went on three."

"You said the race would start on the count of three. I merely followed instructions."

His scowl deepened, and she giggled. He tickled her in the side, and she danced out of reach. Flirting had never come naturally, but with Bennett, it felt right. Like the kiss they'd shared earlier.

Emilia knew it wasn't smart to get closer to Bennett. It would only make it harder when she left. But seeing him held at gunpoint yesterday brought home the stark reality of their lives. Every moment was a gift, and she was wasting them. Bennett Knox was a good man. He made her feel cared for and cherished. Emilia had never had that before. She wanted to hold on to it, even if it was only for a little while.

Metal clanged as Bennett opened the gate. Sheriff King's truck was sitting at an angle on the dirt road. The rumble of a vehicle heading their way snapped Emilia into work mode. A dark blue SUV pulled to a stop. Malcolm was behind the wheel. His gaze clashed with Emilia's and a shiver raced down her spine at the malevolence in his expression.

Bennett moved closer to her. Protective but not overbearing. Although Emilia could handle Malcolm, it was nice to have the support. Sheriff King said something to his son before getting out of the vehicle. Malcolm sped off.

"Bennett, Emilia." Sheriff King strolled over and

shook each of their hands. A Band-Aid covered a bruise on the back of his hand, the wound probably caused by an IV. "Thank you for meeting me. First, I want to apologize for my behavior last night. I started a new medication yesterday, and it interacted badly with another one of my pills. I honestly remember little of what happened, and was horrified to learn I held you at gunpoint. I'm very sorry."

Emilia's heart was moved by his humble apology, and she sent up a prayer of thanksgiving. Many things could've gone wrong—from Randy hitting someone while driving in his condition to accidentally shooting Bennett or her.

Bennett nodded. "I'm glad you're okay and no one was hurt."

"Thank you, son." Sheriff King focused on Bennett before turning to Emilia. "It's no secret I haven't always seen eye to eye with the two of you. I've been arrogant, and the good Lord has taught me a painful lesson."

To Emilia's shock, Randy's chin trembled. Tears shimmered in his eyes. "I was wrong about Derrick. Kathy Rose's death is on me and I want to help you with the case in any way I can."

Emilia wanted to believe the sheriff was sincere. She hoped he was. Yet, a small part of her wondered if Randy's change of heart had anything to do with his son being a suspect.

Bennett tucked his thumbs in the pockets of his jeans. "We'd appreciate any help you can provide. Let's start with Malcolm. Is he Derrick's brother?"

"No. Malcolm's birth parents aren't from Fulton

County. There's no way they are brothers."

"Why didn't Malcolm simply tell me that?"

Sheriff King removed a package of cigarettes from his jacket pocket. "He should have. Malcolm is worried about being linked to Derrick. The man is a serial killer. If people even thought they were related, it could damage his good reputation. Not to mention his business and position on the city council."

"We aren't interested in spreading gossip," Emilia said. "We only want to get to the truth."

"It doesn't matter. Investigations are never ironclad. Leaks happen. With the most recent murder in the news, people would assume Malcolm had something to do with it, even if he's innocent. Blood ties still matter in Fulton County. It's wrong, but that doesn't change the way people feel."

Emilia didn't agree, but then again, she hadn't lived in Fulton County. Maybe his assessment about the townsfolk was right.

Randy lit his cigarette with a trembling hand. Nerves? Or a side effect of Parkinson's? Emilia couldn't tell.

"My son has an alibi for the night Kathy Rose died," Randy said. "He was in Houston attending a conference. Malcolm's attorney will send Sheriff Wilson the details about it. Y'all will verify Malcolm was there and mark him off the suspect list."

Convenient. If Malcolm had an alibi all this time, then why the runaround? Again, Emilia hoped this was a simple misunderstanding.

She pulled out the photograph of Alice with Derrick and Henry. "When I went to turn off your vehicle last night, I found this."

"That's the other thing I wanted to discuss with y'all." Sheriff King took a drag and blew out the smoke. "After I came home from visiting my wife's family, I started going through my notes on the Alice Nelson case. Bennett, do you remember I mentioned she attended a party on the night she disappeared?"

"I do."

"That's a picture from the party. Somehow that photograph ended up in my personal notes instead of the case file." He pointed to Henry in the picture. "This guy is Henry Stillman. He and Derrick were close friends. Henry was also Alice's boyfriend."

Emilia's mind whirled with the new information. "The case file identified John McInnis as Alice's boyfriend."

"Naw. I think they dated for a spell, but it wasn't serious. If you're looking for Derrick's partner, I'd start with Henry. When I was investigating Alice's disappearance, several people told me Henry and Derrick were best buddies. Hung out together quite a bit."

"Did you ever question Henry about Alice?"

"I tried, but he took off at the same time she did. No one knew where he went. Someplace in Louisiana, I think." He took another drag. "People said Alice went with him. I figured she'd pop back up when she tired of him."

Except Alice never returned.

Emilia stuffed her hands in her pockets. She pictured the whiteboard in her mind. There was a year gap between Alice's death and the next murder. If Henry killed Alice, did he disappear from town to evade being caught? Once the case went cold, he could've moved back to Fulton and begun killing women from the surrounding counties.

"Henry Stillman lives here now," Emilia said. "Do you know when he moved back?"

The sheriff cocked his head. "Uhhh, I'd say Henry returned to town about a year after Alice went missing. You'd have to ask him to be sure."

"When he returned did you question him about Alice's disappearance?"

"I did. He claimed to know nothing about it. By that time, the trail had gone cold. I had my suspicions Henry was involved, but I couldn't prove it."

Emilia suspected he hadn't worked hard enough. Anger heated her cheeks, but she tamped the emotion down. The sheriff had made many mistakes, but beating him over the head with them would get her nowhere.

She switched gears. "What about John McInnis? Was Derrick close to him?"

"His boss? I think they were friendly, but nothing more than acquaintances." Randy tossed his cigarette down and snuffed it out with the heel of his boot.

Emilia lifted the photograph. "Where did you get this?"

"Pardon?"

"The photograph." She kept her tone easy and light.

"Where did you get it?"

"I don't rightly remember. Probably from one of Alice's friends."

Sheriff King was lying. Bennett sensed it too. His gaze narrowed. "Did Malcolm attend this party?"

"I doubt it. My son was never much for parties." Randy fiddled with his car keys. "Like I said, if you're looking for Derrick's partner, I'd start with Henry. When I get back to the house, I'll pull all my notes about Alice's disappearance and drop them off at the sheriff's office."

Emilia nodded. "Appreciate it."

"If you have any other questions, let me know. And thanks again for last night."

He ambled to his truck and gave a wave before driving off. Emilia watched his truck disappear around the corner. "Do you get the feeling we were being manipulated?"

"Yeah, Malcolm was definitely at that party, and I bet that picture is his." Bennett removed his hat and raked a hand through his hair. "I can't tell if Sheriff King is trying to simply protect his family's reputation, or if there's something more to it."

"Let's head to town and check in with Claire. Maybe she's reviewed the surveillance video back from the diner where Kathy Rose worked. I'd like to know which of our three suspects—Doug, Malcolm, or Henry—were patrons." Emilia tapped the photograph against her hand. "Alice and Kathy's cases are linked. The first murder and the last. Somewhere a thread ties them together. We just have to find it."

TEN

Bennett held open the door to the sheriff's department for Emilia and then stepped in behind her. Phones were ringing off the hook. Several deputies were manning a hotline for tips. It smelled like coffee and stale pizza.

Claire, looking haggard and exhausted, waved Bennett and Emilia back to her office. "It's a mad house here. How many reporters did you have to wade through to get in?"

"Five," Bennett said, shutting the office door behind him. "But there were more television trucks parked in front of the courthouse entrance."

"The story's been picked up by the national media. I've got the mayor and most of the city council popping in for checkups." She picked up a coffee mug from her desk and sniffed the contents before taking a swig. "Okay, enough about my silly problems. Let's get down to business."

Claire sat in her chair and flipped to a page in her notebook. "The bullets taken from Bennett's truck weren't a match to any crime. So that's a dead end. The only fingerprints recovered from the poinsettia plant given to Emilia at the park belonged to the little boy. There was nothing on the notecard. Killer was smart enough to use gloves. Another dead end."

"What about the composite sketch?" Emilia asked, pulling a wrapped package from her purse. She pushed it across the desk. "Bennett's mom made blueberry muffins. I grabbed a few for you."

"You're an angel. I haven't eaten since..." She frowned. "I can't remember." Claire opened the wrapping and breathed deep. "Oh, these smell amazing. Hold on, let me get some coffee. Composite sketch is right there under that folder."

Emilia located the composite and groaned. "You've got to be kidding me."

Bennett leaned over her shoulder to look. The man was wearing a hat and sunglasses. A scarf covered the lower half of his face.

He sighed. "That could be anyone."

"The killer is willing to take risks, and smart enough to minimize them."

Claire bustled back into the office with a fresh cup of coffee. "Sorry, I neglected to ask if y'all want anything."

"Don't worry about us," Bennett said. "We know where the break room is. Sheriff King told us Malcolm has an alibi for the night Kathy died."

"He was at a legal conference in Houston. Malcolm is refusing to sit down for questioning, but his attorney has sent me the information."

"Houston is only four hours away. He could've driven back, killed Kathy, left her body in the park, and returned for the conference."

"I had the same thought." Claire broke off a piece of blueberry muffin. "One of my deputies is in contact with the hotel. We're going to check the surveillance footage to verify Malcolm was there all night."

Bennett grinned. He liked working with Claire. She was smart, dedicated, and willing to go the extra mile.

"What else did Sheriff King tell you?" Claire asked, popping the muffin piece in her mouth.

Bennett ran through their earlier conversation with Randy. "I want to believe he's genuinely sorry and trying to help, but the meeting felt contrived. Especially since Malcolm could've cleared this up with a simple conversation."

"I don't think everything Randy said was a lie." Claire tossed the muffin wrapper into the trash. "I followed your advice, Emilia, and went through the surveillance video from the diner where Kathy worked for the last two weeks. Malcolm never stepped inside. However, Henry did."

Bennett's heart skipped a beat. Was this the break in the case they were looking for? He prayed it was.

Claire opened a folder and removed a series of photographs. "These are stills taken from the video. As you can see, Henry is a regular. All the employees know him. They describe him as friendly and easygoing, a generous tipper. Henry often requested Kathy to be his waitress."

Emilia leaned over the desk and pulled one of the photographs toward her. In it, Henry was talking to Kathy. The time/date stamp indicated it was one week before her death.

"He created a rapport with her," Emilia said. "So later, when he approached her in the dead of night while she was walking home, Kathy wouldn't be worried. She had no reason to run or be scared. To Kathy, Henry was one of her customers and a nice guy."

"He could've created a ruse to kidnap her." Bennett picked up on Emilia's train of thought. "Like a broken-down car. Or that he was hurt. Something that would've caused Kathy to get close enough so he could shock her with the stun gun."

Claire nodded. "I've got several deputies knocking on doors in the neighborhood, asking questions along those lines. A neighbor must've seen something." She pulled out another photograph. "There's more. You'll never guess who Henry went to the diner with from time to time."

Emilia's eyes widened. "John McInnis."

"Yep."

Claire set the photograph down on top of the others. John and Henry were seated at a booth eating. Kathy was refilling their drinks.

Bennett glanced at the time/date stamp. "This is two days before Kathy disappeared."

"It's the last time Henry or John went to the diner. I did some digging, and it turns out the two men are related. Henry is married to John's sister."

Emilia sat back in the chair. "What's the relationship like between John and Henry? Could Henry have put Kathy's body on the running trail John uses to frame him for the murder?"

"Possibly. I asked around quietly and there's bad blood between John and Henry. It stems from an old business dealing they had together. I don't have all the details yet, but I'm working on it." She wrinkled her nose. "I'd ask John, but I don't think he'll tell me the truth."

Emilia nodded. "Sheriff King said Henry and Derrick were good friends. John never mentioned it. He's protecting his brother-in-law."

"That's not unusual for family members. Even though there are issues between the two men, John and Henry hang out. I can't trust that John will keep quiet about our suspicions. I don't want to tip Henry off that we're looking into him for the murders."

Bennett rocked back on his heels. "There may be another way to approach it."

"How?" Emilia asked.

"John indicated Malcolm may be involved in the murders. Let's use that." He removed the photograph from his pocket. "This picture taken on the night Alice disappeared has Henry in it. We can ask if Malcolm was at the party."

She drummed her nails on the desk. "Let Henry think we're focused on someone else as Derrick's partner. Yes, that could work. We should do it at his house since it's less confrontational that way. And I should be there."

Bennett wanted to argue, but Emilia was right. The killer had an obsession with her. If Henry was their man, then it would be hard for him to hide it while she was close by.

He sucked in a breath as a realization slammed into him with the force of a sledgehammer. Emilia and Henry had met in foster care. He'd tormented her. Bennett had always believed the killer became fixated on Emilia during the first investigation, but that assumption could be wrong.

If Henry was the killer, he may have been obsessed with Emilia for decades.

They were getting closer to the truth, Emilia could feel it. She strategized with Bennett about the case during the twenty-minute drive across the county. It wasn't possible to rule out John or Malcolm, but Henry was turning into their top suspect.

Bennett turned onto a small country road. A quaint wooden bridge appeared, big enough for only one car to pass through at a time. Down below, was a river. The water rushed and tumbled, threading its way through a few rocks.

Emilia stretched in her seat to get a better view. "This is so pretty."

"I've always liked it. When we were teenagers, during the summers, we used to raft down this river." Bennett gestured to the left. "There's a dock up that way where you can get in. The hardest part is carrying your raft back to the starting point."

His tires rumbled over the wooden bridge and then the GPS directed them to turn. A small ranch-style house came into view. It needed a fresh coat of paint, but the flower beds were meticulous and the porch railing was wrapped with red ribbons for Christmas. A sedan sat in the carport next to a black truck.

Emilia exited Bennett's vehicle. The wind whipped her hair and snaked down the collar of her jacket to chill her skin.

Henry came around the side of the house on a riding lawn mower. He raised a hand to block the sun from his gaze. A flash of recognition passed across his features when he spotted Emilia. He killed the engine on the lawn mower and closed the distance to them on long strides.

"Emilia, hi." Henry removed his work gloves. Grass clippings clung to his pants and dirt stained his shirt. "And Bennett, right? I'd shake your hand, but I'm filthy. Planted a bunch of new flowers in the backyard and it shows."

"That's all right." Bennett smiled. "Sorry to drop in, but we'd like to ask you a few questions about an investigation we're conducting. Is there someplace we can sit and talk?"

Henry's brow furrowed. "Uh, sure. I have a sunroom in the back. If you don't mind, we can circle the house using the yard. I don't want to track all this dirt and grass clippings inside."

"Not a problem."

The backyard was as pretty as the front. Bushes and flowers were artistically laid out in a gorgeous garden surrounding a sunroom. A mermaid fountain sprayed water into a tiny pond complete with goldfish.

Emilia stopped to read the inscription on the metal bench next to the walkway. "With God all things are possible."

"Matthew 19:26." Henry paused on the walkway and turned to face her. "That scripture saved my life. I was on a bad path in my teens and twenties. In fact, I owe you an apology for the way I treated you when we were in foster care together, Emilia. I wanted to say something at the hospital, but it was awkward." He flashed a smile. "I suppose this is, too, but better awkward than not at all."

Doubt wormed its way into the certainty Emilia had formed about Henry's guilt. His apology seemed genuine, and Henry hadn't been arrested since his twenties. Did they have the wrong man?

She glanced at Bennett and saw her own confusion mirrored in his expression.

They followed Henry into the sunroom. It was decorated in muted colors, with soft love seats and simple end tables. A poinsettia sat on the coffee table.

Emilia's heart skittered.

"Henry?" A woman appeared in the doorway leading to the house. She was dressed casually in jeans and a sweater, and her dark hair was pulled back into a bun. "What's going on?" Her attention flickered to Emilia and Bennett. "Everything okay?"

"Fine, dear. This is Texas Ranger Bennett—" Henry paused. "Sorry, I forgot your last name."

"Knox. Bennett Knox."

Emilia forced a friendly smile, hoping to put the other woman at ease about their surprise visit. "I'm Special Agent Emilia Sanchez."

"Nice to meet you. I'm Jackie Stillman."

Jackie's resemblance to the murder victims was unmistakable. She was slender and pretty, but her hair color didn't appear natural. Her eyebrows were much lighter, indicating she was actually blonde. Why had she dyed her hair chocolate brown? For Henry?

Emilia's heart beat faster as her gaze darted to the poinsettia on the table, then to Henry. Their eyes clashed. For a moment, the sunroom disappeared, and she was back in the cabin. Panic swelled in her chest and the scar on her arm burned. Her hand drifted to her sleeve, but instead of touching the mottled skin, her fingers tripped over metal. The bracelet Bennett had given her. Her thumb traced the cross charm and her breathing settled.

She was okay. Bennett was with her. So was the Lord.

The panic attack subsided, leaving her weak-kneed.

Henry was still watching her, but his expression was confused. "Emilia, are you okay? You look pale?"

"Fine." The word came out on a croak and she cleared her throat. "I'm fine."

But she wasn't fine. The panic attack had been swift. She hadn't had one in months. Was it seeing Henry again that triggered it? Or was the stress of the last few days catching up with her? Emilia couldn't tell, and it was unsettling.

Bennett placed a hand on the small of her back and she leaned into the touch, letting his presence ground her. His words from earlier this morning filtered through her mind. She *was* strong and resilient.

This case wouldn't break her. She wouldn't let it.

———

The couch cushion dipped under his weight and Bennett pitched forward to stop from sinking in deeper. He cast a glance at Emilia, concern nipping him. It seemed like she was on the verge of a panic attack a few moments ago. Whatever it was seemed to have passed. The color had returned to her cheeks.

Henry sat on the couch across from them. The sunlight hit on the scar along his lower lip. "What can I help you with?"

"We're looking into the disappearance of Alice Nelson. It may be connected to a recent murder in town."

"Kathy Rose, yes, I know." His shoulders slumped. "I knew Kathy. Not well, but my wife works days and I work nights. We don't have dinner together due to our schedules so I would often pop into the diner. Kathy was a nice lady, always had a smile for everyone."

"And Alice Nelson? Did you know her?"

"I did. She and I were good friends. In fact, the last time I saw her was at a party we attended together."

Bennett took out the photograph and showed it to Henry. "Was this taken at the party?"

"It was." Henry took the picture and studied it. A flicker of sadness and regret crossed his face. "I was supposed to drive her home, but I got plastered at the party and passed out. Woke up the next morning lying on the bathroom floor with little recollection about what had happened the night before."

"So the last time you saw Alice was at the party?"

He nodded. "She disappeared sometime that night. I've racked my brain trying to remember who she left the party with, but I can't."

Emilia pointed to the picture. "Is it possible she left with Derrick?"

"I don't know." Henry's knee jiggled with energy. "I'm ashamed to say it, but I'm an alcoholic. In those days, I started drinking before ten in the morning, and by nine at night, I couldn't pronounce my own name. Hit rock bottom when I went to jail for my second DUI. Afterward, I started attending Alcoholic Anonymous meetings, became a Christian, and turned my life around."

Jackie came into the room with glasses of iced tea.

She distributed the drinks and then took a seat next to her husband.

Henry showed her the picture. "Bennett and Emilia are looking into Alice's disappearance. You were at the party that night. Do you remember who she left with?"

Jackie's complexion paled. "No. I left before her."

Bennett set his iced tea on the table. "Can either of you tell me if Malcolm King was at the party?"

Henry nodded. "He was. I distinctly remember him by the keg." He glanced down at the photograph in his hand. "Come to think of it, Malcolm and Derrick had words that night. It was a silly fight over an insult, but it blew over quickly."

"Were they friends?"

Henry hesitated. "Here's the thing. Malcolm and Derrick were friends, but they only hung out together at parties. Sheriff King didn't like Derrick—I don't know why—and Malcolm avoided irritating his dad."

There was a ring of truth to Henry's observations. He seemed honest and willing to help. Then again, the killer was smart and adept enough to hide in plain view.

Henry's brow creased. "I'm confused. What does Alice's disappearance have to do with Kathy's murder?"

"We believe the two cases are connected." Bennett pointed to the picture. "Derrick was working with someone when he committed those murders last year. His partner killed Kathy and we think they may have been working together as far back as seven years ago. Alice may have been the first victim."

Jackie gasped, and the glass in her hand crashed to the tile floor. It broke into a thousand pieces.

Henry hopped up as liquid splashed his pants. "Honey, goodness, are you okay?"

"What a silly goose I am." She shook from head to toe. "I'm going to get some paper towels to clean this up."

Emilia shot Bennett a glance and rose from the couch. "I'll help you."

The two women disappeared into the house.

Henry patted the photograph in his hand with the sleeve of his shirt. "I'm so sorry. It got a little wet."

"Don't worry about it. It's a copy." The original was locked in an evidence locker at the sheriff's office.

Henry sank to the couch. "Derrick and I were close friends once. Drinking buddies. After I got sober, I encouraged him to get clean too. Invited him to AA meetings, to attend church with me. He refused. I'd hoped God would fill the void in his life, but he turned to evil and darkness." Henry blinked and raised his gaze to Bennett's. Tears shimmered in his eyes. "Do you really believe Alice is dead?"

"It's a strong possibility."

He ran a hand over his face and sniffed. "I let her down. I'm responsible."

Henry was teetering on the edge. Bennett had never suffered from addiction, but he knew there were triggers. He didn't want to push Henry into drinking. "No, sir. The killer is the only one responsible."

"I'm gonna need to go to an AA meeting tonight." He blew out a breath. "I'm sorry I can't be more help. Like I said, I was drunk. But you can ask my brother-in-law, John. He was also at the party. John lives right next door—"

The screen door creaked open. John stood in the entrance, a scowl on his face. "My ears are burning. What are you saying about me, Henry?"

"Oh, hey, John. Have you met—"

"We have." John came inside and the screen door slammed shut with the force of a bullet. A flush colored the cheeks above his thick beard. "Ranger Knox. What are you doing here?"

A tension Bennett couldn't decipher filled the space. He stood. "We're following up on Alice's disappearance and Kathy's murder. Henry explained Derrick and Malcolm were friends, but it was a secret."

Henry showed him the photograph. "You took this, remember?"

Jackie and Emilia came back into the room. Jackie ignored her brother and busied herself with cleaning up the broken glass and spilled tea. Bennett had the impression that Jackie was looking to disappear. The woman seemed terrified, but he couldn't make heads or tails of it.

He glanced at Emilia. Her expression was placid.

"Yeah, I remember taking the picture." John crossed his arms over his chest. "And yes, Malcolm and Derrick were good friends. Like I said, they were more than friends. They were brothers."

Henry's mouth dropped open. "What?"

"Malcolm denies it," Emilia said.

"Of course he does." John snorted. "Sheriff King

never liked Derrick to begin with. They won't claim him now that he's a serial killer. It would ruin their precious reputation. But mark my words, Malcolm's involved in these murders."

"Hold on, John." Henry's face reddened. "You can't go around making accusations about people like that."

"I can if it's true."

ELEVEN

The night air was crisp and clean. Emilia breathed deep and used her toe to send the porch swing rocking. Christmas lights from the Knox house made colorful spots on the cement. Through the large living room window, the tree sparkled.

The door opened and Bennett's family poured out. Liz ran up to Emilia. The little girl's eyes were shining. "We're going to see the Christmas lights in town and have hot cocoa. Are you coming?"

"No, honey." Emilia wanted to join them, but the shooting incident stopped her. Being with Bennett's family was risky. On the ranch, there was security. Beyond the fence, anything could happen. "But tomorrow, I want to hear about your adventure. Make sure you remember all the details."

"Okay." Liz grinned and then hugged Emilia. "See you later."

Bennett and his dad approached. Zeke patted Emilia's shoulder. "Call if you need us, darlin'. We won't be far."

The fatherly touch and simple term of endearment brought sudden tears to Emilia's eyes. She blinked them back, embarrassed by her reaction. Her emotions were running too close to the surface today.

"We'll be fine, Dad." Bennett joined Emilia on the swing, handing her a cup of apple cider. "Have a good time."

With a final wave from the vehicles, the rest of the family left.

Emilia took a sip of the warm apple cider and sighed. "This is amazing. I have to get your mom to give me the recipe."

Bennett wrapped his arm around her shoulders and she leaned into him. His chest was hard, and faintly, through the fabric of his jacket, she could hear the steady beat of his heart. The scent of his cologne wrapped around her like a blanket. It was soothing.

He pushed with his leg and the swing rocked gently. "What were you thinking about out here by yourself?"

"The case. What else?" She sighed. "Specifically, I was thinking about Jackie. She was terrified but refused to tell me why. In the kitchen, I gave her my card and told her to call me if she wanted to talk. But it's bugging me. I got the impression she was scared of someone. But who?"

"I know. We've got three suspects and no clear evidence pointing to anyone."

She tapped her fingers against the mug. "We're

missing something. How does the crime tie into the killer's history?"

"What do you mean?"

"The murders are very specific. The cuts on the victims, painting their nails, the poinsettia. It's ritualistic. Why does the killer do it? Who does the victim represent? A girlfriend? A mother? That's the missing element. And Alice is the key. She knew all the suspects. It started with that party and her disappearance."

"Marcy Nelson, Alice's grandmother, comes back from her trip tomorrow. We can ask her."

Emilia nodded. She was tempted to curl up next to Bennett and forget about the world for a while, but there was something else they had to talk about. She gripped her cup. "Bennett, I need to tell you something. This morning, when we kissed...."

Heat flooded her cheeks. The words she'd practiced saying wouldn't come out of her mouth as nerves tightened her chest.

"It meant something to me too." He slipped a hand in hers. "I have strong feelings for you, Emilia."

Inside, her heart soared to hear the words spoken aloud. It confirmed her instincts and made her long for more than she could have. She squeezed his hand. "The same. I care about you, Bennett. My feelings are stronger and deeper than I'd like to admit to." Her chin trembled. "But I don't want to hurt you."

"Because you can't live in Fulton County."

"No, I can't."

Bennett pushed the swing with his foot, sending

them into a gentle swaying motion. The Christmas lights on the house winked. Emilia never talked about what she'd been through after escaping from the cabin and returning home, but with Bennett, things were different.

She took a deep breath. "After the attack last year, I suffered from bad nightmares. It was hard to leave the house, go to work, attend church. I saw a therapist and spent time in prayer. Once the therapist cleared me to go back to work, I told myself it was over. I didn't have to think about it anymore. And that's what I did. I blocked everything out, dove back into my work, and tried to create a normal life."

"Did it work?"

"I thought it did. Spending time with you, being around your family...it makes me realize how lonely I've been."

For decades. She'd been alone for decades.

"Growing up wasn't easy. My parents, well, they weren't really parents. My mom was a drug addict from the time I was little. My dad was in and out of prison. Foster care was better, but I never had anything permanent. In eleven years, I moved thirty times. That's thirty new homes and new families. It meant changing schools and adapting to other kids in the house. It was constant upheaval."

Bennett was quiet. He kept the swing in motion, his hand wrapped around hers, gently urging her to keep talking.

"To survive, I kept moving forward. I blocked out or ignored anything that stood in the way of my goals. After the attack last year, I did the same. It seemed like the best way to get my life back." She sighed, long and low. "Now I'm back here, surrounded by all the memories of what happened, trying to stop a new killer. It's unchartered territory for me. I can't block it out like I want to."

She lifted her head from his chest and shifted on the seat to face him. "Bennett, I want to tell you I'll be fine when this is done. But I can't. After we catch this killer, my instincts are to turn around and never come back to this area of Texas again."

"I don't blame you." Bennett reached up and tucked a strand of hair behind her ear. "But I'll be honest with you, Em. It breaks my heart to hear you've been going through this alone. I wouldn't wish that on anyone."

Tears flooded her eyes, and Emilia blinked rapidly to keep them from falling. "Bennett, you have me crying again. Ugh, twice in one day."

He took the mug from her hand and set it on the porch railing along with his. "Maybe you need to cry. A part of you must know I'll catch you when you fall."

"I do know that."

"Then let me." Bennett took her hands in his. "God puts people in our lives for a reason. You've tried going through this on your own. It hasn't worked. Now try walking through it with me."

She wanted to. She trusted Bennett with her life. The problem was her. She didn't trust herself not to cut and run once the case was over. "What if I can't stay? What if it's too much for me?"

"Then it is." Bennett squeezed her hands. "I want

you to be happy, Em. I hope that's with me, but I'll understand if it's not. There's a lot of history between us, and most of it is wrapped up in serial killers. It's not the most romantic beginning to a love story."

"No." She took a deep breath. "You aren't scared?"

"I was, but not anymore. My sister gave me a good piece of advice. She told me to put my faith in God and trust that He will guide me to the right place." Bennett cupped her face. "I'm going to do that. I hope you will too."

He bent his head and kissed her. Bennett's mouth was soft, his touch gentle, but it lit Emilia up within. She clung to his broad shoulders and let the world fade away. Here, in his arms, she was safe. She was cared for.

When the kiss ended, Emilia was breathless. She brushed his mouth with hers one more time before backing away. A light over Bennett's shoulder caught her attention, but it was too bright to be the normal glow from a house, even with Christmas lights.

She frowned. "Is that a fire over there?"

She pointed and Bennett turned. He shot up from the porch swing. "That's my neighbor's house and, yes, it's on fire."

Bennett gripped the steering wheel as his tires bounced over the dirt road leading to his neighbor's home. Emilia was on the phone with 9-1-1. The fire department was located in the center of town, a good twenty minutes away. Mark and Valerie were married with three young kids. Had they all gotten out of the house safely?

Bennett's pulse roared in his ears as the house came into view. Flames shot up to the sky. The wind changed and smoke blew directly in his path, temporarily blinding him. He deviated from the unpaved driveway onto the grass.

Emilia hung up. "Fire trucks and EMS are on the way. Fifteen minutes ETA."

His headlights swept across the yard as he pulled to a stop a safe distance from the house. Valerie, her face streaked with tears and soot, raced toward the vehicle. In her arms, she carried a crying infant. Two other children trailed her, wearing pajamas. Everyone was barefoot.

Bennett bolted from the vehicle and intercepted them. "Are you all okay?"

"Mark is still inside. He wasn't in bed when I woke up." Valerie's voice broke off as a sob choked her.

He turned to Emilia. "There are blankets and a first aid kit in my truck."

Bennett didn't wait for her response. He took off across the yard. The heat from the fire seared him. Rather than going in the front door, he circled the house, searching for another entrance.

The back door was closed. Bennett twisted the knob. Smoke poured out, but there weren't flames in this part of the house. "Mark!"

No answer. Bennett covered his mouth with his shirt and crossed the threshold into the mudroom. Keeping low, he raced into the kitchen. The smoke made his eyes burn and tear. He blinked to clear them. A figure in slippers lay on the tile floor.

Mark.

Bennett grabbed his neighbor and hauled him to the back door. Coughs overtook Bennett as he tumbled into the yard. He sucked in big breaths of fresh air and used his shirtsleeve to clear away the fresh tears pooling in his eyes. "Mark, are you okay?"

His neighbor didn't answer. Bennett took a last swipe at his eyes and blinked. Mark's arms were secured behind his back with zip ties. Duct tape sealed his mouth and a bloody gash crossed his forehead. He was conscious.

Bennett ripped the tape from the other man's mouth. "Mark, what happened?"

"I don't know. Someone hit me in the head and I passed out—"

A bloodcurdling scream sent Bennett's heart into overdrive. It'd come from the front yard.

No, no, no. It was a trap.

Emilia!

Bennett took off for the front of the house, yanking his weapon from the holster. His boots slid on the grass as he rounded the corner and his vehicle came into view. Kids were seated inside covered in blankets. A first aid kit lay on the grass, contents spilled. Valerie, her mouth hanging open, was staring at the tree line in horror.

He didn't stop to ask questions. Bennett sprinted for the tree line. There was another road a short distance away. He couldn't let the killer get to a vehicle with Emilia.

Branches slapped his face and tugged at his clothes. His heart thundered and his lungs burned from the smoke. Sweat mingled with the soot on his face.

Please, Lord. Please don't let me be too late.

The sound of someone crashing through the woods caused Bennett to deviate from his path. He caught sight of a strange figure. It took him half a breath to realize it was a man carrying a woman over his shoulder.

Emilia was struggling. She arched her back but didn't use her hands. They were probably secured behind her.

"Police!" Bennett yelled, but his voice, damaged by the smoke inhalation, barely carried. "Freeze!"

Bennett didn't bother raising his weapon. From this distance, in the dark, there was too great a risk he would accidentally hit Emilia. Instead, he poured all his energy into running. His only hope was closing the distance between them and tackling the killer. Adrenaline surged through Bennett's veins.

Emilia screamed and then arched her back again.

The killer stumbled, dropping her. He glanced over his shoulder, but his face was covered by a ski mask. Still, he must've heard or seen Bennett because he abandoned Emilia on the ground and took off.

Chest heaving, Bennett skid to a stop next to Emilia. He dropped to his knees at her side.

"Go." She jerked her chin. "I'm okay. Go!"

He spared one second to touch Emilia's cheek.

Then Bennett raced after the attacker.

TWELVE

Emilia peeled her eyes open and winced. Her head pounded like someone was banging it with a metal pot. The stark white walls of the hospital room spun. She took a deep breath to settle her stomach before opening her eyes again. Better.

She turned her head. Bennett was dozing in the chair next to her bed. His clothes were wrinkled and mud-stained. Bristles covered the sharp curve of his jaw. Emilia vaguely remembered waking in the middle of the night and Bennett comforting her through a nightmare. He'd been with her all night, watching over her, keeping her safe.

He stirred and opened his eyes. Bennett smiled softly. "Hey, Em. How do you feel?"

"Like someone jolted me with a stun gun, whacked me in the head, and tried to kidnap me."

Bennett kissed her forehead. Then he poured her a cup of water from a carafe on the nightstand. "Here."

She fumbled with the button to put her bed into a sitting position, and braced for a wave of nausea, but it never came. That was good. She'd been diagnosed with a concussion in the emergency room last night. Sleeping must've helped.

Emilia took the cup from Bennett and sipped. The cool liquid soothed her raw throat. She crooked her finger, indicating Bennett should come closer. He did, and Emilia brushed her lips against his. The bristles on his chin scraped against her skin.

His green eyes warmed, and the look melted her insides. She didn't need Bennett to say what he was feeling. Last night had been terrifying for both of them.

And it wasn't over yet. The killer was still out there.

"Any news?" she asked.

Bennett perched on the edge of her bed. "Not much. Mark was able to give a statement last night, but he didn't see anything helpful. A masked man broke in, knocked Mark out, and then set fire to the house. Valerie never saw the intruder. She was sleeping and woke up when the fire alarms went off. Their house is destroyed."

Emilia's hand tightened on the plastic cup, crumpling it. "It was a well-planned ruse to get to me. And a dangerous one. The whole family could've been killed."

"My ranch security is too difficult for the killer to get through, so yes, he set the neighbor's house on fire knowing we would render aid. I also don't think it was an accident my family was gone when it happened. It was the only way to ensure you would be with me, instead of my dad or Grayson. The killer must've been watching for the right moment."

"He's patient and smart." She leaned against the pillow. "And he's not going to stop. I'm worried, Bennett. He failed last night. What will he do next?"

"Let's pray he's holed up somewhere nursing his injuries. I'm almost sure one of my bullets grazed him, although it wasn't enough to keep the killer from escaping in his truck. Claire is monitoring hospitals in the surrounding areas in case someone comes in with a bullet wound."

The next few hours were a blur of activity. Emilia had another MRI to verify her concussion was healing enough she could go home. Sage brought extra clothes and toiletries to the hospital. A shower, some coffee, and breakfast went a long way. By the time Emilia signed the discharge paperwork, she was feeling like herself again.

A knock came on the open door of the hospital room and Claire walked in. Dark circles shadowed the skin under her eyes, but her hair was in a neat bun and her uniform ironed. She carried a folder in one hand.

Emilia's heart sank. "You aren't bringing good news, are you?"

"I'm afraid not. We have a new missing woman." Claire pulled out a photograph. "Gretchen Knight. Twenty-six. She was kidnapped in the early-morning hours while opening the bakery."

Bennett took the picture. Emilia drew closer to look over his shoulder. Gretchen was dark-haired and pretty with a smattering of freckles across her nose.

An indescribable rage filled Emilia and heated her blood. "The killer failed with me so then he took Gretchen."

"It would appear that way, although I suspect he was stalking Gretchen for a while. The bakery doesn't have great surveillance cameras, but a black truck was in the parking lot. It matches your description, Bennett, of the vehicle the killer escaped in last night. Gretchen had complained to her boss about the same truck hanging around the bakery for the last several weeks."

"Did the camera catch the license plate?" he asked.

"Registered to a vehicle in Dallas. The plates were stolen six months ago, so that's a dead end." Claire rubbed her eyes. "But there's more. Henry Stillman and his wife are gone."

Emilia sank onto the bed. "What do you mean gone?"

"Henry and his wife, Jackie, both called into their respective jobs and took immediate vacation time. No one has seen them since yesterday afternoon."

"What about John? He's their next-door neighbor and Jackie's brother."

"He doesn't know where they are." Claire's mouth tightened. "But I don't believe him. John is a property manager. He has access to numerous rental homes, some of which are standing empty at the moment. Henry and his wife could be hiding out in one, but proving that is difficult."

"Or they could be halfway to Mexico," Emilia said. "Jackie was terrified yesterday when we discussed Alice's disappearance. She knew something but was too scared to say what. Maybe she told Henry, and they left town. Where was Malcolm last night?"

"At home, alone. However, we were able to verify his alibi for the night Kathy was killed. He's not our man."

"And John?"

"Also home alone. But he doesn't have a black truck registered in his name and he consented to a search of his home. We didn't find anything." Claire frowned. "Henry, however, owns a black Ford truck. His wife may have been terrified because she put two and two together yesterday during your questioning."

Bennett nodded. "She figured out her husband was the one who killed Alice, along with Derrick."

"After you left, she may have confronted him. It set off a chain reaction. I'm afraid Jackie's life may be in danger. Or she may already be dead."

"Have you gotten a search warrant for Henry's house?"

"I don't have any direct evidence tying Henry to these murders. No fingerprints, no DNA, and no witnesses. All I have at the moment is that he owns a black truck and took a surprise vacation. It's suspicious, but not enough to convince a judge to give me a search warrant for Henry's house. I've put a BOLO out on Henry's truck and his wife's sedan—"

"Wait, they took two cars?" Emilia frowned. "That's weird."

"I agree, but both vehicles are missing from the carport. Every available law enforcement officer in the state is looking for the Stillmans as well as Gretchen."

Nothing about this was making sense to Emilia. Henry had been so convincing about turning his life around. Had he fooled her? It certainly seemed that way. And hadn't she almost had a panic attack in Henry's house? She'd excused it as a momentary blip, but it might've been something more. Maybe her subconscious was signaling to her that Henry had been the other man in the cabin on the night she escaped.

Emilia took the photograph from Bennett. Gretchen's smile was bright, her dark eyes sparkling. A cross hung around her neck. Only twenty-six years old. Her family must be worried sick, with good reason. Gretchen was in the hands of a madman.

"We're on a ticking clock." Emilia's voice was hollow, even to her own ears. "If we don't find Gretchen in the next twenty-four hours, she'll be dead."

Bennett placed a hand on Emilia's elbow as she navigated the walkway up to Marcy Nelson's home. "You should be at the ranch, in bed, which is exactly what the doctor ordered. I can interview Alice's grandmother on my own."

"Her house is on the way. It's silly to drive to the ranch only to turn around and come back." Emilia punched the doorbell. "Gretchen doesn't have that kind of time. We need evidence linking Henry to these murders. Alice's grandmother may be the key."

Bennett smothered his irritation. Emilia was only

doing her job. He knew that. But her complexion was pale and she was still unsteady on her feet. Concussions weren't something to play around with. Not to mention there was a killer hunting her.

Henry Stillman. The man had fooled Bennett by talking about overcoming his addiction, turning his life around with Christ. Perhaps that was the point. Henry could hide in plain sight by appealing to people's sense of compassion and passing himself off as a man of faith. He wouldn't be the first killer to have done so.

Emilia pressed the doorbell again, and it warbled out a tune. Shuffling came from inside the house and a voice called out. "Coming. I'm coming."

Moments later, the door swung open, revealing an elderly woman. Her beehive hairdo added height to her petite frame. She blinked at them from behind oversized glasses. "May I help you?"

"Yes, Mrs. Nelson, I'm Texas Ranger Bennett—"

"Oh, of course, dear." She stepped back and opened the door wider. "Joanna's boy. I know your mother well from her work at the soup kitchen. Please come in."

Bennett stepped over the threshold and removed his hat. He'd combed his hair and cleaned himself up as best as he could at the hospital, but dried mud still clung to his boots. He slid them off and left them at the door. The inside of Marcy's home was immaculate, and he didn't want to ruin the white carpet.

He half listened as Emilia introduced herself. Marcy escorted them into the living room.

"I'm so sorry I wasn't here when you first came by a

few days ago. I was visiting my sister in Florida. She's just moved and has been after me to join her. I lost my husband two years ago to cancer. She's worried I'm lonely." Marcy paused to take a breath. "Can I get either of you anything? I have coffee or tea."

"No, ma'am." Bennett joined Emilia on the couch. "But thank you."

Marcy settled into an armchair. "Bennett and Emilia, I have to say, thank you so much for looking into Alice's case. It's been a long time since anyone has shown interest." She removed a tissue from her sleeve and dabbed at her eyes. "Alice was my only grandchild. Not a day goes by I don't think of her."

Seven years. Alice had been missing for seven years and her family had no answers about what had happened to her. It made Bennett angry. For Mrs. Nelson. For the other families who lost loved ones because a killer hadn't been caught.

Marcy swiped the tears from her cheeks. "Forgive me. My emotions are running away from me. My daughter died just six months after Alice disappeared. A broken heart, I think. When Alice didn't come home for her mother's funeral, I knew something was very wrong. To be frank, I knew she was dead. Alice and her mother were close." She took a deep breath. "What can I do to help?"

Bennett removed a photograph from his jacket pocket. "This picture was taken on the night Alice disappeared. What can you tell us about her relationship with Derrick Jackson?"

"Oh, to my knowledge Alice wasn't friendly with Derrick. Now, this other young man, Henry Stillman is a different matter." She pointed to Henry in the picture. "Henry and Alice were very close, since they were little kids."

Emilia leaned forward. "I wasn't aware Henry grew up in Fulton County."

"Oh yes, dear. Until he was ten, I'd say. That's when his father's drinking got out of control and social services removed Henry from the home. They couldn't find his mother. She'd left when Henry was just a baby." Marcy shook her head and her beehive wobbled. "Shameful. Anyway, Alice reconnected with Henry after he moved back to town. They had a special bond. I think it was the tragedy that did it."

"Tragedy?"

"Henry's aunt was murdered. Horrible thing. The killer was the poor woman's boyfriend. It seems he was jealous she'd moved on. Henry, Alice, and some other neighborhood kids were in the backyard playing when it happened. They didn't hear anything, but I believe Henry was the one who found her."

Emilia passed Bennett a glance. He knew exactly what she was thinking. This could be the link they need to prove Henry was the killer. The murders were ritualistic. Was he reliving the scene he'd discovered at his aunt's house?

If that was the case, why hadn't Sheriff King put two and two together a long time ago? Or maybe he had, which is why he insisted they look into Henry.

Bennett's mind raced as he pulled out his cell phone to text Claire. "Do you know the name of Henry's aunt? And the year the murder took place?"

"The year was 1999. I don't remember the aunt's name." Marcy tapped her temple. "My mind's not what it used to be. But we can look it up. Come with me."

She rose from the armchair. Bennett and Emilia followed her down the hall into a bedroom converted into an office. File cabinets lined one large wall.

"My husband was a newspaper reporter for decades. He kept every one of his stories along with all the research." She pulled open a drawer marked with the correct year. "Let me think...the murder happened in the winter. I remember that specifically."

She flipped through the files with agonizing slowness. Bennett was tempted to push Marcy out of the way and do it himself. From the way Emilia's hands twitched, she was thinking the same.

"Here we are." Marcy removed a folder. "Rachel Stillman. That was her name."

Papers fluttered out of the folder and slid across the carpet. A crime scene photo landed near Bennett's foot.

Marcy gasped. "Oh, my. I'm so sorry. Sometimes my husband was able to get police photographs. He was very close to Sheriff King."

Bennett barely heard her. He picked up the picture, his movements slow.

The woman in the crime scene photograph was lying on a tile floor. Cuts covered her arms. Defensive wounds, judging from their angle. She'd been stabbed multiple times in the chest.

Henry's aunt was dark-haired and pretty. Her nails were painted red. A poinsettia had tipped over next to her, the bloom mingling with the blood on the floor.

Emilia took the picture from him and studied it before lifting her gaze. "Is this enough to get a search warrant for Henry's house?"

He nodded. "I'll call the judge myself on the way over there. Let's go."

THIRTEEN

Bennett flew down the country road toward Henry's house. Rain pattered the windshield and thunderclouds hovered overhead. Claire was preparing the search warrant, and the judge had promised to sign it electronically the moment it was ready. Several deputies were also en route although they were at least twenty minutes behind Bennett.

He prayed they would find something at Henry's house, some indication of where he was holding Gretchen.

Emilia studied the photograph of Henry's aunt. "How on earth did Sheriff King miss this connection? The crime scene is similar enough, he should have realized it when the first murder happened last year."

"I had the same thought. Sheriff King insisted Henry was involved when we spoke to him the other day, but failed to mention the aunt's murder. Either it was a horrible oversight on his part or..."

His voice trailed off as a horrifying thought solidified in his mind. No. it wasn't possible.

Was it?

"Bennett, we never verified Sheriff King was on vacation with his wife when the first murder happened." Emilia turned to face him. "He knew Derrick. Several people told us Sheriff King had done everything to prevent Malcolm from interacting with Derrick. What if that's because Sheriff King and Derrick were partners?"

Bennett wanted to tell her the idea was insane, but he'd been wrong so many times during the course of this case, he wouldn't reject anything outright.

"During the initial murders, Derrick took most of the risk," Emilia continued. "He kidnapped the victims, the killing happened in his cabin, and the women were probably buried on his property. Maybe that was by design."

Bennett glanced at her before locking his eyes on the road. "Derrick was expendable. A potential fall guy. Except the killer didn't stop when Derrick died. He started up again."

"Because he failed. It all comes back to that. The killer can't stand losing, and that's what happened last year when I escaped. His compulsion to finish what he started is impossible for him to ignore, even if it means taking greater risk in exposing himself."

Bennett gripped the steering wheel tighter. Sheriff King was stubborn and never wavered once his mind was made up. His personality was completely in line with what Emilia was describing.

"You said the murders were ritualistic." Bennett

increased the speed of his windshield wipers. "How does that fit if Sheriff King was working with Derrick? Doesn't it make more sense that Henry was working with Derrick?"

"Not if the killer was smart enough to create a second backup plan. Someone he could frame if Derrick got caught or was killed." She lifted the photograph. "The killer could've been inspired by this scene and recreated it, knowing it would point investigators to Henry."

Emilia's cell phone rang, interrupting their conversation. She rummaged in her purse and unearthed it. "Sanchez."

A woman's voice poured out. Bennett couldn't make out the words, but her tone was frantic.

Emilia put the call on speaker. "Where are you, Jackie?"

Henry's wife. Bennett instinctively slowed the vehicle, so he could listen to the call.

"We're at my house." Jackie's voice was thick, as if she'd been crying. "Please, hurry. He's going to kill me."

"Who?" Emilia asked.

"I was so scared when you were at my house asking questions," Jackie continued as if Emilia hadn't spoken. "I couldn't tell you the truth. Please, hurry. He's mad and I'm terrified."

Bennett pushed on the gas again. He held up his hand, showing Emilia five fingers to indicate they would arrive at Henry's house within five minutes.

"We're on our way there right now," Emilia said to Jackie. "How did you get back to your house?"

"Henry took the back roads. He's upset the police are looking for us." Jackie inhaled and then her breathing became frantic. The sound of banging came over the line. "Oh, no. Please..."

"Jackie, what's happening?"

"He's going to kill me. He's—" Jackie screamed.

It was the sound of pure instinctive terror.

Bennett's heart jumped into overdrive. He pushed the gas down, and his truck surged forward. Windshield wipers swiped at the water pouring on the truck but did little to clear the glass. The thunderstorm was in full force.

Emilia called in to dispatch. Backup was ten minutes behind them.

Ten minutes. So much could happen in that time.

The country road leading to Henry's house appeared. Bennett barely tapped the brakes as he took the turn. Emilia whispered a prayer and gripped the roll bar. Her cell phone rattled in the cup holder.

The bridge appeared. Faint and distorted in the rain. Bennett flipped on his brights to warn oncoming drivers. The beams arced across something unfamiliar.

A woman lying in the road.

"Bennett!" Emilia screamed.

He swerved.

His tires rolled over something and exploded. The truck spun out of control, the wet road as slick as an ice rink. The bridge loomed large in his windshield, and then glass shattered. Pain ricocheted through him, arcing up his leg. Bennett had a momentary vision of the puff of his airbag before his face slammed into it.

———

Emilia groaned. Cold air and icy rain soaked her clothes. Her entire body hurt.

She opened her eyes and blinked. The front end of Bennett's truck had broken through the bridge's guardrail. The creek below rushed and trembled, encouraged by the raging thunderstorm.

Emilia's deflated airbag rose up to block her view. She shoved it away. "Bennett?"

Silence. She turned her head, wincing at the excruciating pain.

Bennett was facedown in the airbag. His hair was soaked from the rain. The water dripped down his face and into the collar of his shirt. Blood, from a wound she couldn't see, mingled with the rain.

"Bennett." Tears pricked her eyes as she fumbled for his neck to feel for a pulse. His skin was ice cold.

She couldn't find a heartbeat. *No, God, no.*

"Bennett!"

He groaned and shifted.

Emilia's heart stuttered and then took off. "Bennett, wake up."

The sound of her voice must have jolted him into awareness. He sat up, his face turning toward her. Pain rippled across his features. "Emilia, are you okay?"

"I'm okay. But you're hurt." She searched with her

hands for her cell phone among the glass shards and broken plastic. It'd been in the cup holder, but it was gone. "Where are you hurt, Bennett?"

She had to keep him talking. He could go into shock.

"My left leg is the worst of it. It's trapped under the steering wheel." He shifted and then winced. "I can't get out."

She glanced behind her at the road. Through the pouring rain, the woman on the road was barely visible.

"Can you reach your cell phone to call for help?" Emilia removed her gun from the holster at her back and checked the magazine. "Tell dispatch about our situation. The deputies need to be warned."

Bennett grabbed her hand. "It's a trap."

"I know, but the woman is still out there. I can't leave her." Emilia leaned over and pressed a kiss to his mouth. Quick and hurried, but it warmed her straight through. "I love you, Bennett Knox."

Emilia didn't give him a chance to say anything. She was on the verge of tears as it was, her emotions running high along with her adrenaline. Shoving the truck door open, Emilia scrambled out. Glass littered the pavement and rain pelted her.

She took two seconds to sweep the area. The thunderstorm made visibility poor. Trees waved in the strong wind. If the killer was wearing black, he could easily pop out from the shadows.

Emilia sucked in a breath and half ran, half loped to the woman lying on the road. Pain shot through her head and her muscles protested each movement. She kept her gun tightly gripped in her hand.

Jackie. The woman had been shot. She was holding her hands over her abdomen.

"I'm here." Emilia ripped off her jacket and lowered herself next to Jackie's side. She pressed the fabric to the wound. "You're going to be okay."

Jackie pulled on Emilia's hands. Her mouth moved, but no words came out.

"Who did this to you?" Emilia leaned down until she was close to Jackie's lips.

Jackie's eyes were wide with fear. "R-r-run."

White-hot pain jolted through Emilia and her muscles clenched as electricity from a stun gun raced through her body. It stopped as suddenly as it started. She tumbled to the ground. Her gun fell from her numb fingers. From a distance, someone was screaming her name.

Bennett. Bennett was yelling her name.

A man dressed in black appeared like an apparition from the woods. He jolted Emilia again. Pain exploded in her body. When the shock stopped, she was as weak as a newborn kitten.

Somewhere in Emilia's mind, she realized his stun gun could be operated from far. The nodes must be in her back, but she couldn't reach them or pull together the power to control her muscles.

Within half a heartbeat, her hands were secure with zip ties. Feet too. The attacker hauled her over his shoulder and jogged over the bridge to a truck. Black. So dark they hadn't seen it in the rain, waiting and watching.

The killer dumped Emilia in the back seat of the extended cab, jolted her again with the stun gun for good measure, and then slammed the door. The truck rumbled to life.

The engine revved. Emilia was thrown against the seat as the sound of crunching metal assaulted her ears. What was he doing?

Their vehicle slammed into reverse and then again raced forward. More metal crunched and then the sound of wood snapping. A terrifying realization cut through Emilia's pain. The killer was ramming his truck into Bennett's, pushing him off the bridge and into the river.

Emilia's mouth moved, but nothing came out. Tears coursed down her cheeks. Her mind could hardly function, but her heart whispered prayers.

A tremendous crash reached her ears, the splash of water.

Then the sound of manic laughter.

"Who's going to save you now? No one, my pet. No one."

FOURTEEN

Emilia drifted in and out of consciousness as the truck rumbled to its destination. She tried to pay attention to the route, but it was impossible, given her condition. The car accident and stun gun had exacerbated her concussion. Nausea threatened and her head felt like it was about to explode. Every muscle in her body ached. But none of her physical ailments compared to the agony in her heart when she thought of Bennett.

His leg had been trapped in the truck. Even if he survived the tumble into the creek—a miracle, for sure—Bennett wouldn't be able to get out of the vehicle. He'd drown. The thoughts and images in Emilia's mind were crippling. Tears dripped off her cheeks onto the carpet.

Emilia fingered the bracelet on her wrist, her thumb running over the cross charm. *Please Lord, I need your strength now more than ever.*

She couldn't think about Bennett. The grief would

overwhelm her, and things were bad enough already. Emilia had to keep it together long enough to rescue Gretchen. It was her sole purpose now.

The truck stopped. Metal rumbled as a garage door opened. The sound of the rain faded when the vehicle rolled inside the garage and the door closed behind them.

Trapped. Emilia was about to come face-to-face with the man from her nightmares. A cold-blooded killer. Panic threatened to well up, but she battled it back.

The rear door on the extended cab opened. Emilia winced at the bright light shining in her face. Rough hands grabbed her, and she tumbled to the concrete floor with enough force to knock the breath from her lungs. Before she had a chance to recover, the killer hauled her up by the hair, twisting her neck so fiercely Emilia feared it would break.

"Walk, my pet."

His voice sent chills down her spine, but she complied. Her knees wobbled and her skull felt like it was on fire. The zip ties binding her hands in front of her cut into the skin at her wrists. She couldn't see the killer's face from this angle.

He forced her through an open doorway into another space. A kitchen? But unfinished. Pipes for the sink and appliances spanned the wall.

He shoved her. Emilia stumbled and fell, sliding across the dirty tile floor. She struggled to get up, but her body—damaged by the trauma over the last day—was slow to comply. The killer chuckled. He grabbed her bound hands and quickly attached her to a thick pipe with more zip ties.

Emilia glanced up. Her breath stalled in her lungs.

John McInnis.

Her muscles trembled as the killer hovered over her. Buried memories flicked through her mind like a horror film, but indistinct and hazy. They'd left her alone, bleeding and tied up, in the cabin. A piece of broken glass had been lodged in between the wooden slates of the floor. She'd used it to cut the ropes binding her. As she'd escaped, John had returned. He'd chased her through the woods.

The trembling in her body increased. "I didn't remember it was you."

He chuckled. "A side effect of the drug Derrick injected you with." John's gaze met hers and he ran a finger over her cheek. "But now we can be face-to-face, my pet, and you'll remember everything. It's better this way. I have some business to attend to and then we can play."

Bile rose in her throat, as the meaning of his words sank terror into her. She swallowed. "Where's Gretchen?"

"I'm so glad you asked. She's here."

Emilia followed the line of his finger. Across the room, attached to another pipe, was Gretchen. The young woman was bleeding from her calf and a cut on her left arm. Light sparkled off the cross hanging from her necklace. Mascara coated the skin under vacant eyes. Gretchen appeared to be in shock.

But she was alive. Emilia needed to do everything she could to keep her that way.

John peeled off his raincoat and dropped it on a plastic chair. He winced. "First things first, I have to change my dressing." He glared at Emilia. "Your stupid boyfriend got in a lucky shot last night."

A folding table held an assortment of items. Antibacterial ointment, gauze, and medical tape sat next to a few takeaway boxes from a popular fast-food restaurant. Emilia's gaze darted around. They were in a house under construction. Large windows on the far side of the room provided views of the surrounding property. A lake, water rippling from the rain, sat in the distance.

"You own Ignite Development." Emilia tugged against the zip ties on her wrist. They held fast. "You bought Derrick's property to hide the bodies buried on it. Is that where we are?"

"We're nearby." John lifted his shirt, revealing a bandage along his rib cage. "This will be the model home for the residential neighborhood. Do you like it?"

She ignored his question. John peeled off the dressing. A nasty wound marred his side. It appeared infected to Emilia's untrained eye and in need of stitches.

John opened a new package of gauze. "Derrick was supposed to take the fall for all the murders, but your escape messed up my plans."

"You should've stopped when he died."

"I couldn't. The work wasn't finished. Trouble was, once the police knew Derrick had a partner, they would look back at the cases and discover Alice was the first."

On the other side of the room, close to Gretchen, was another table. It was covered in knives.

Emilia's heart pounded in time with her head. John wanted to talk and she would use that to her advantage. It bought her time to come up with a plan.

She licked her lips. "You loved Alice, but she wasn't interested in you. She wanted Malcolm, didn't she?"

John slammed a hand down on the table. His cheeks were red above the line of his beard. "She was short-sighted. I could have given her everything, but she threw it all away."

"You convinced Derrick to give her a ride home from the party."

"She wouldn't take one from me. I scared her." John ripped off a piece of tape with more force than necessary. He used it to secure a new bandage to his side. "Derrick and I became friends after he started working for me. He hated Malcolm almost as much as I did."

"Because they're brothers. You were telling the truth about that."

"Malcolm didn't want to have anything to do with Derrick. Originally, we were going to frame Malcolm for Alice's murder, but..." A slow smile stretched across his face. "It was amazing killing her. I didn't want to stop. Neither did Derrick. He liked watching. It was the perfect partnership. We devised a plan to keep going, but we had to be smart about it, so the police wouldn't catch on."

They had been smart. Killing at Christmastime, taking women from different areas. It was only when the bodies started showing up in public parks law enforcement caught on to what was happening. And even then, Sheriff King had prevented the task force from getting the full picture. His incompetence had cost lives.

The zip ties binding Emilia's wrists wouldn't give. She had nothing to cut them with. The table of knives was too far away for her to reach. "Whose idea was it to use the murder of Henry's aunt as inspiration?"

"Mine. I was there when she was killed, playing with the other kids in the yard. Everyone thought it was Henry who found her, but it was me. My fascination with death started that day and grew from there." John lowered his shirt. His eyes sparkled. "As much trouble as you've caused me, my pet, it's been worth it. I'm almost glad you escaped."

He'd sent her the poinsettias. John was on the trail when they found his victim in the park. He wanted to be interviewed afterward so he could point Emilia toward Malcolm. It'd all been a game to him. Terrorizing Emilia fueled his sick desire.

Anger heated her cheeks. "You won't get away with it, John. Law enforcement was on the way to Henry's house. They'll find your sister on the road."

"She'll be dead by then. Her husband is at my house, tied up. My stupid sister finally realized I was the killer. Can you believe Henry showed up and asked me to confess? Turn myself in? What a joke. I'll frame him for the murders instead."

John was insane, but in an utterly scary way. He planned and plotted his horrors.

"I missed having Derrick watch me kill. An audience just makes things more interesting." John ambled over to Emilia. He leaned down until his nose was in her hair and breathed in. "Now I have you to watch me, my pet."

Disgust roiled her stomach. Emilia swiped out with her leg and knocked John off his feet. He landed on the floor in a heap. She kicked again, her heel landing in his side, smashing into his injury.

John howled in pain and rolled away. The table with the knives tumbled down as he knocked into it. Curses flew from his mouth.

Emilia frantically tugged on the zip ties, using her weight as a counterforce. She needed to break them. There was no chance of survival if she didn't get free. The pipe rattled with the force of her movements, but the zip ties held.

John groaned. He lumbered to his feet, holding his side, but stayed out of striking distance. His face was red with pain and anger. "I'm going to make you pay for that, my pet."

Lightning streaked across the sky followed by a window-rattling boom. The lights went out, plunging the room into darkness.

Thank you, Lord. Every minute helps.

John cursed again. Emilia couldn't make out his facial features, but his large form stumbled to the other table. Fabric crinkled as he tugged on his raincoat, muttering something about circuit breakers. He exited using a door attached to the kitchen. A light flickered on as he flipped on his cell phone flashlight.

Emilia waited until it disappeared from view. Then, again, she frantically yanked on the binds around her wrist. The zip ties refused to snap.

Her eyes were adjusting to the darkened room. Gretchen's small form was tucked into a ball. The knives from the table were scattered on the floor near her.

"Gretchen, I need your help. My name is Emilia and I'm a police officer. We've been looking everywhere for you."

Silence. Emilia tugged on the zip ties again. "I know you're scared and hurting. But I need you to pick up one of those knives with your free hand and cut yourself loose."

She waited one heartbeat. Two.

A sob broke the silence. Gretchen's body shook. "I can't. He'll hurt me more."

The sound of the other woman's fear ate at Emilia. But they had a small window of opportunity. She prayed to God for the right words. Something inside of Emilia went still and quiet. Her fingers found the cross on the end of the bracelet Bennett had given her.

"This is the most terrifying moment of your life, Gretchen. I know that. But in your darkest moments, God is with you. You're never alone. And sometimes He sends someone to help you. Someone who will get you through."

How could she have been so blind? God had heard Emilia's prayers for healing. He'd sent her exactly the help she needed to mend the broken pieces of herself.

Bennett. His love, dedication, and gentleness were the support she needed.

And Emilia was what Bennett needed too. Hadn't she restored his faith in love? Her honesty, her strength, and resilience meant she stuck around when things got hard. She wouldn't leave him at the first bump in the road.

God had been guiding them all this time. And he was guiding Emilia now.

Tears clouded her vision and thickened her voice. "God has put the two of us in this room to help each other, Gretchen. We have a fighting chance, but we have to work for it. Say a prayer and pick up a knife. Please."

The only sound was Gretchen's sobs and the rain hitting the windows. Then the scrape of a knife against the floor. Gretchen grunted as she cut the tie on her wrist.

Emilia's heart leapt. Her gaze darted to the back door. No sign of John, but he was close. There was no time to waste.

Gretchen tried to stand and fell. She cried out in pain.

"Don't walk," Emilia said. "Just crawl to me. You're doing great, Gretchen."

Gretchen maneuvered across the distance between them. Her breathing was rapid and tears fell down her cheeks. "I'm coming. Hold on."

She used Emilia's body to steady herself and then cut the zip ties. Emilia's hands flew free of the pipe and she caught Gretchen before the woman fell. Lightning lit up the room followed by more thunder.

There was no sign of John. Where was he? Probably somewhere in the backyard. That's where most homes had the circuit box, if it wasn't in the garage.

They would use the front door to escape.

Emilia wrapped Gretchen's arm over her shoulders. "Here give me the knife."

She took the weapon. It was a double-edged blade. Emilia tested the weight and adjusted her grip. "Let's get out of here, Gretchen."

She half pulled, half carried Gretchen across the kitchen floor. The house had been framed but the drywall was missing. The front door was forty feet away. Emilia glanced over her shoulder. The hair on the back of her neck stood on end and everything inside her urged speed.

Emilia tried to pick up the pace. It was difficult with her injuries and Gretchen's.

Twenty feet.

Windows rattled with the wind.

Gretchen screeched. The woman's whole body shook.

"It's okay." Emilia didn't stop her forward momentum. "Keep moving. I'll protect you."

Ten feet.

The door flung open. A dark shadow stood back-dropped against the rain.

Gretchen screamed and reared back, nearly taking

Emilia to the floor. She scrambled to put herself in front of the other woman as John lunged toward them.

Emilia lashed out with the knife. It caught John on the throat and he howled. She followed it up with a second swipe that cut his arm. He reached for her, and she dodged. Her head spun as a wave of nausea slammed into her. Emilia's vision clouded.

Gretchen grabbed her arm. Emilia sucked in a breath and held on to the other woman. Her dizziness passed. She lifted Gretchen to her feet. They scrambled to the other side of the room.

John roared with anger. Emilia felt rather than saw him coming after them.

Back door. They needed to get to the back door.

Something moved on the opposite side of the glass a moment before the back door swung open. A dark form appeared holding a flashlight and a gun. "Police! Freeze!"

Sheriff deputies in bullet-proof vests poured into the room from different entrance points. Several grabbed John and tackled him to the floor. He screamed in frustration.

They were safe. Emilia sank to her knees, relief making her head spin again. Gretchen clung to her, sobs racking her body.

Emilia wrapped her arms around the other woman and rocked her like she would a child. "We're safe. It's over."

Claire appeared at Emilia's side. Her gaze swept over her. "Get EMS in here. Now!"

"I'm okay. It's Gretchen who needs help the most."

She grabbed Claire's arm. Emilia's throat tightened making it difficult to force out any words. "Bennett? Is he—"

"He's alive." Claire's mouth twitched. "And madder than a hornet because I wouldn't let him participate in the takedown due to his injuries."

"Guys, move." Bennett's voice carried across the room. "Or I will knock you out of my way."

It was the first time Emilia had ever heard Bennett raise his voice. Fresh tears rolled down her face. Claire pulled Gretchen aside so the EMS could attend to her. Emilia stood on shaking legs.

Deputies parted, creating a path for Bennett. He was limping and blood soaked the left leg of his pants. A homemade tourniquet encased his thigh. He was wearing someone else's jacket. Scrapes covered his face and hands, and he smelled like a mixture of fish and rainwater.

He'd never looked better.

Emilia flung herself into his arms. He held her tight and then kissed her, making her heart race and her head spin again. Cheers and claps went up from the deputies standing around them. Bennett pulled away long enough to remove the jacket he was wearing. He wrapped around her shoulders before pulling her into his arms again.

"You're alive." She placed a hand over his heart, feeling the steady beat. "But you need a hospital."

"I need you more." He kissed her forehead. "My leg came free when the truck fell into the water. I was able to escape just as Claire arrived on the scene." Bennett found the bracelet on Emilia's wrist with his fingers. "We were able to track you using the GPS charm."

He'd saved her life. Again.

Emilia met his gaze, and oh, she could drown in his green eyes. They held warmth and desire. They held forever. "I love you, Bennett Knox."

He cupped her face in his hands. "I love you too."

FIFTEEN

One year later

Bennett weaved his way through the gathering at his parents' home. Friends and extended family were partaking in food and chatting in small groups. The wedding rehearsal had gone off without a hitch. Tomorrow, Bennett would marry the woman of his dreams.

Speaking of, where was Emilia? He hadn't seen her for the last five minutes.

Claire, almost unrecognizable out of uniform, stood next to the Christmas tree. She was one of Emilia's bridesmaids. The two women had grown close after the investigation. Cadaver dogs located the fourteen women buried on Derrick's former property, including Alice. John pleaded guilty to murder and would spend the rest of his life in prison.

Gretchen had recovered from her injuries. She went

back to school and was currently getting her master's in Colorado. She'd sent a beautiful crystal cross as a wedding gift with a kind note.

Bennett joined Claire. "Hey, have you seen my fiancée?"

"Not in the last few minutes, but I'm sure she's around here somewhere. Maybe in the kitchen?"

"Good idea. I'll check."

He crisscrossed the room into the kitchen, but Emilia wasn't there either. Bennett slipped outside into the cold night air and circled the house to the front porch. Emilia was standing on the driveway. Christmas lights from the roof played across her face.

It'd been Emilia's idea to get married two weeks before Christmas. Bennett had been surprised by the suggestion, certain that the month would hold difficult memories, but she insisted.

Was she having regrets?

"Emilia, what are you doing out here all by yourself?" He drew closer and saw the tears streaking her cheeks. "You're crying."

He cupped her face and swiped at the water on her skin, concern shooting through him. "What's wrong?"

"Nothing." Emilia caught his hands. She smiled, her eyes crinkling at the corners. "Don't worry. They're happy tears. Grateful ones. I prayed for so long to belong somewhere, to have a family. And now, tomorrow, I'm going to become Emilia Knox."

He scanned her expression but found no trace of

sadness. He kissed her gently. "I like the sound of that. Emilia Knox."

"So do I." She stepped into the circle of his arms and rested her head on his chest. "It's a dream come true."

It hadn't come easily. After John's attack, Bennett offered to move to Austin for Emilia. He'd realized that while his life and his family were in Fulton County, his heart was anywhere Emilia was.

She refused his offer. Instead, Emilia found a cottage in town. She'd insisted that family was important. She wanted their future children to have grandparents living close by. Bennett and Emilia spent the next year dating, their love growing each day. Therapy eased Emilia's anxiety. Time paved the way for new memories, good ones this time.

From this angle, the inside of the house was visible. A Christmas tree twinkled in the corner. Bennett's family and some lingering guests were gathered around the piano. Everyone was singing carols.

That's why Emilia was standing here. She could see her family.

She sighed against his chest, and Bennett hugged her tighter. "I love you, Em."

"I love you too." She pulled back to look him in the face. "Do you remember when you carried me out of the woods? Do you recall what you said to me?"

He remembered every harrowing second. There were only two times in his life he'd ever been that afraid. The second was racing to the house where John was holding

Emilia, praying that she would be alive when he got there.

"Of course." Bennett brushed a hair off her forehead. "I called you a fighter."

"I want you to know, sweetheart, that I'm going to fight for our marriage every step of the way. When things are hard, I'm going to dig in. It's you and me. Forever."

Her words warmed him straight through. Bennett already knew Emilia wouldn't give up and walk away, but it was nice to hear the words, anyway. "I promise the same."

He bent his head and kissed her. Emilia's lips were soft and warm, and held the lingering taste of hot cocoa. Bennett's heart skittered and his knees went weak. She had the power to undo him and always would.

The screen door creaked open, interrupting their kiss.

"Emilia," Sage called. "Stop canoodling with Bennett. You have your whole life to do that after the wedding tomorrow. It's time to go."

Bennett rested his forehead against Emilia's and groaned. "Go away, sis."

Sage chuckled. "No can do, big brother. The last of the guests are leaving and Emilia is coming home with me. A bride needs her beauty rest."

Emilia kissed him one last time. It was quick but full of promise.

"I'd better go, or she'll just come down here and get me."

He reluctantly released her. "Sweet dreams."

"See you at the altar tomorrow." She winked. "I'll be the one in the poufy white dress."

Bennett chuckled. Emilia ran up the porch steps and Sage wrapped an arm around her waist. The two women went back inside the house.

Through the window, Bennett watched as everyone hugged Emilia goodbye. She was loved.

By him, most of all.

ALSO BY LYNN SHANNON

Available Now

Vanish

Ranger Protection

Ranger Redemption

Ranger Courage

Ranger Faith

Ranger Honor

Coming 2021

Ranger Loyalty

Would you like to know when my next book is released? Or when my novels go on sale? It's easy. Subscribe to my newsletter at www.lynnshannon.com and all of the info will come straight to your inbox!

Reviews help readers find books. Please consider leaving a review at your favorite place of purchase or anywhere you discover new books. Thank you.

Made in the USA
Columbia, SC
11 June 2021

39850986R00109